MISADVENTURES OF PRINCESS SYDNEY

by CHRIS MINICH

chris
MINICH
children's author

Snoqualmie WA 2016

740L

Cover Design by Michelle Fairbanks
Edited by Toddie Downs
Illustrations by Janelle Minich

This is a work of fiction. Names, characters, places, brands, media, and
incidents are either the product of the author's imagination or are used
fictitiously. Any resemblance to similarly named places or to persons
living or deceased is unintentional.

Library of Congress Control Number: 2014920646

For Beautiful

This book is dedicated to the love of my life. I fall more in love with you each and every passing day. My life began when I met you, I haven't looked back since.

ACKNOWLEDGMENTS

When it came time to write acknowledgments for this book I thought about my mom and award shows. She always asks — and probably still does — why do people say, "I would like to thank"? To her, if you want to thank someone you should just do it. I love you Mom, thank you for all your support. I miss you Dad. Your memory lives on. To all my family and friends, whether you know it or not, you have all helped shape who I am and a little piece of each of you is with me every day. That's a gift I cherish.

This book would not be possible without an amazing team of talented and inspiring people. To my editor, Toddie Downs. I could spend the rest of the acknowledgments thanking you. With your guidance and suggestions, we turned a little story about a dog named Sydney into an awesome book that I will forever be proud of. To Michelle Fairbanks, who knocked it out of the park with the cover. To my multi-talented wife, who conveyed the heart and soul of the characters in this book like no one could through her wonderful illustrations. To Kara Roberts, who came across the country to be part of our doggy photo shoot. You captured the heart of our heroine in all her digital glory. If pictures are worth a thousand words, I need to start on more thank you cards. Thank you! To my mentor extraordinaire, Tess Thompson. You believed in me and in what I was writing. You also taught me if I could "show, don't tell" I'd have a story on my hands. I'm honored to call you a friend and to quote Wayne and Garth, "I'm not worthy."

Finally, this book would not be possible without the love and support from the most beautiful woman on God's green earth. I love you! My wife is amazing. If you're lucky enough to know her, you know this to be true. Everything good I will ever do stems from her, including this book. I thank God for her each and every day. Thanks God! One fall evening I was struggling to put a character into a situation for a homework assignment when she suggested, "Why don't you make the character Sydney?" Sydney is our little cockapoo. She is full of energy, charisma and mischief, and truly this man's best friend. She is also my muse and inspiration for this book. Our family would grow to include our "Terrier Surprise," Buddy. He is not Sydney's best friend but he'll be yours, no questions asked. All that's required is a little love—he has plenty to give. Together, we make up our little family. One last thank you. Thanks, whoever, wherever you are for finding and reading this book about a cockapoo named Sydney. I hope you have as much fun reading it as I did writing it. Come to think of it, I want to read it again. Okay, let's begin.

CHAPTER 1

SYDNEY

"TIME TO GET UP, SYDNEY." Sleeping is so awesome. Well, it is until your mom comes into the room and tries to pull you from your golden slumber. I'm a princess after all and I wake and sleep on my own time and terms. "Sydney," Mom says again in a more stern voice, "You're burning daylight." The shades are still drawn with just a little morning light peeking through. Burning? I think Mom is a little dramatic. I don't enjoy this time of day. I prefer staying on the bed, contemplating another nap, safe in my spot that I've kept warm for the last few hours. Can't I sleep a bit more? I don't have to be to work for a little while longer. I run a tight ship here at the house and no once comes or goes without clearance from this hound. Besides, why do I have to get up if he gets to continue sleeping? As I turn, I see my dad still asleep on the bed.

This is so not cool. Welcome to my morning.

As she walks up to the bed, my mom puts her hand lightly on my dad's chest as he begins to wake. They bring their lips together in an awkward embrace called kissing. Yuck. Who came up with the unpleasantness? I love my mom and dad, but they have it all wrong. I prefer the time honored tradition of licking the face of the one you love to show affection. Perhaps it's a dream, I mean nightmare. I try opening one eye thinking I will right this wrong I've just seen. No such luck, my eyes are already open. Laying my head back on the bed, I enjoy a few more minutes of that dream-like state.

Mom walks over to me and asks, "Sydney, do you want a tummy rub?" Ah, one of my favorite questions of all time! I see what she's doing here. Trying to wake me up with the promise of love and attention. She so gets me. Of course I want a tummy rub. I may be sleepy, but have I ever turned down a tummy rub? Answer: no. This is something my mom has done ever since I was very little. I consider myself a lady first and foremost, but when talk of a tummy rum comes up, I will do just about anything for one. If you haven't had one, I highly recommend it.

Oh, here she comes. The tummy rub is about to start. Mom scratches and pets my tummy. She is a master in this field. Dad however, not so much. Mom is able to make my legs tingle and twitch. Whenever Dad tries, my legs shimmy and shake. Just to be clear these are not the same thing. Mom always manages to find that itchy spot that I can never seem to reach. She's great. As she does this, I get so excited that my back leg starts twitching and I can't do anything to stop it. Honestly, I don't even want to. Just when I think, it can't get any better, Mom starts scratching my chin. I love this part so much I wrap my paws around her hand so she knows I don't want her to stop. Mom takes the hint and the excitement continues.

During all the fun, my dad finally decides to sit up and slowly turns and places both of his feet on the carpeted floor. After listening to all the creaking and cracking from his morning stretches, he heads into what Mom and Dad call the bathroom. Interesting, this bathroom. When it comes time for me to take care of my business, my parentals— mom and dad—let me outside into air which is occasionally cool, wet or frigid. Yet they get their own special room which is pleasant and dry. Pays to have two legs, I guess. As my mom heads back out of the room, I jump off the bed and saunter over to this bath area. The tile is cool on my feet and I can now feel that light shining down on me from the overhead skylight. My dad turns on the shower and prepares to clean himself for the day.

Dad's cleaning ritual is quite the ordeal. With the water running–yes, you heard me–he steps into this box protected by two panes of glass on the outside and tile on the interior. He then gets all wet from the water–um, why? Then he uses some kind of sudsy liquid to clean his thinning hair. I don't like it when water falls on my fur. It feels like I've gained ten pounds (of water weight) and I just end up spending hours trying to do as Taylor says and shake it off. Besides, damp is not a good look for me.

While Dad showers, I lay on one of the soft, luxurious floor mats in the bathroom and proceed to clean myself. First, I use my tongue to get to my paws and remove any grit from the previous day. Next, I move my front paw up over my head to brush out my ears and straighten the fur on top of my head. Ah, that does it.

It is here that I see my reflection in the glass pane. For just waking up, I clean up pretty well. The glass doesn't lie. I've still got my looks and as always, a cute and spunky attitude. With my golden caramel coloring, soft fur and long flowing eye lashes, I can tell you, I'm a pretty sharp looking cockapoo. Mom says I'm a mix of cocker spaniel and poodle. Dad says I'm a little bit country and a little bit rock and roll. Hint, he's from a faraway place called the nineteen seventies. I say I'm the perfect mix of lovable and totally awesome. And I do like the bathroom; I enjoy sitting here where the rug backs up to the shower and I can feel warmth coming through the glass. Guess there is a benefit to Dad's cleaning ritual after all.

After my dad turns off the shower and uses a fluffy towel to dry himself off, I stand right in front of the door, eager to greet him for the first time today. Do I tease my dad from time to time? Yes. Is he the punchline for my humor? Yes. Is he the best thing that ever happened to my mom and me? Yes! My dad is the best; just don't tell him I said that. Where was I, oh yes, greetings. Now comes my favorite part. Carefully, Dad opens the shower door and reaches down to pet me on my head. Ah, heaven.

My dad usually takes a few minutes from this point to dress. With just the right amount of white and caramel soft fur on my back, I'm perfectly comfortable, but Mom and Dad like to wear these things called clothes. Seems like a waste to me. Once dressed, my dad proceeds to spend some of his precious time brushing his teeth. Have you heard of it? I don't mind him doing it so much, but do not like it when my mom periodically decides I need my teeth brushed as well. She applies tooth-paste on the brush and claims that it "tastes like chicken." FYI, it does not. Mom then inserts the brush into my mouth and tries to clean my teeth. She may have a goal here but mine is to simply bite down on the brush to make it stop. The gritty feel, the long stick with what feel like little needles rub-bing back and forth on my teeth and gums–thank you, but no. My parentals seem pretty smart, so I don't understand why this needs to occur. I'll be honest with you, I don't know what a cavity is, but Mom tells me brushing will help prevent them and keep my teeth strong. No one ever looks at my teeth and gums, though. I get that she's trying to help me, since I would have trouble doing it myself, but seriously, I would prefer to not be involved with tooth brushing at all. I don't know how Mom and Dad do it every single day, usually twice. Yeah, no!

Finally, Dad turns out the light in the bathroom, and after loading his pockets full of all kinds of interesting things I'm not supposed to know any-thing about, he heads toward the bedroom door. Please, I'm no stranger to what Dad carries around in his pockets. For instance, this morning, Dad put keys in one of them. I love keys. They jingle, jangle, jingle, and they're fun to play with as well. Sometimes I try to put them in my mouth, but Dad doesn't really like that too much. Especially after an incident playing with said keys, where I had a little too much fun and the horn went off on Dad's vehicle. Once! One time! So, suddenly now, keys are off limits? Whatever.

Another fact about pockets. On special occasions, a tissue will end up in one of them. Oh, don't get me started on tissues. So light, so soft against my fur, so–

Dad interrupts my thoughts. "Come on Sydney," I hear him say. Fantasizing on tissues will have to wait. If Dad follows the normal schedule, it's now time for breakfast. Score. I dart out of the room and catch up to him in seconds. Four legs vs. two–you do the math.

Dad stops in the hallway to talk to Mom. Hello, I'm hungry here. Need some assistance. What, more kissing again? I walk over to Dad. "Excuse me," I bark, "I don't mean to be rude, but I'm hungry." Every day, I patiently wait at the top of the stairs while they kiss yet again. If they had a plane to catch, we'd already be downstairs, but if I'm hungry, we wait an extra minute or two.

"Okay, Syd," Dad finally says to me, "but I bet your brother is hungry as well. Let's not forget him." Oh, my bad. I was having such a great morning I must have skimmed over the part about the fourth member of our household. My brother, Buddy. Did I neglect to mention him? Yup!

"Come on, Buddy," Dad calls out to him. From out of the shadows, the four legged mongrel emerges, bounding down the hallway. A-panting he will go, a-panting he will go... A couple of quick steps down the hall and heavy breathing begins. Hey, Mom, I think we have a good candidate for teeth brushing. Buddy pushes his way in front of me and tries to climb up Dad's leg.

I have to move back because now his tail is swatting me in the face. An example of one of the many reasons he wasn't mentioned until now. I'm still hungry and don't have time for this sidebar to my morning.

"Attention!" I bark, causing everyone to stop what they're doing. "Breakfast, remember?" I head to the stairs. I thought handling my brother was easy. Dad is a piece of cake. Yum, cake. Is it too early in the morning for cake? Probably!

Moving along. Going back to the occupant, or my brother, as Mom and Dad refer to him. Although I prefer to not even look in his general direction, for the sake of this chapter I will say only that we share the same room, eat our meals at the same time, chase similar squeaky toys when thrown our general directions, and, oh yeah, vie for our parentals's affection.

Never mind him. For now, I'm on a mission. Breakfast, people, let's go. I need some yum yums.

CHAPTER 2
SYDNEY

MAKING IT DOWNSTAIRS FIRST, I quickly dart out of the way as my brother comes charging down behind me and at the last moment, like he does every morning, forgets he needs to stop. He slides past me on the hardwood floor, feet trying to gain some sort of traction, clumsily arriving in the kitchen. Graceful he is not. As if showing their age, the parental units take their sweet time descending from the second floor, one step at a time, mind you, and finally arrive in the kitchen. Dad walks past me, stopping for a quick pat on my head, and ventures over to the back sliding glass door. Ah, I see what he is doing, changing the play by calling an audible.

"Come on, you two," he says, and opens the door, allowing us to go outside. As we walk on by, he reminds us, "Take a break." If memory serves, and it usually does, he stole that line from Mom. This is Dad's way of telling us it's time to let nature take its course. Overshare? Well, it's a long tale. Ha, that never gets old. After taking care of things, I get a minute to roam around and I see Mom and Dad kissing yet again. Ugh. I'm hungry, but nothing will kill a raging appetite quicker than this continued display of tenderness, as no child wants to watch their parentals being all—what's the word—affectionate toward each other. Gulp. Hold it back, breathe, focus, focus... ooh, bunny rabbit at twelve o'clock! Time for my morning exercise.

Nothing gets me more amped up, not even making new friends when people come over to our house for a visit, than when I see one of those white fluffy cotton balls skirting around in my backyard. I always try and make their acquaintance, but they never seem to want to hang out for very long. Perhaps it's my approach? Let me just say, they're missing out, because I've been told I'm pretty awesome. I feel a great day coming on.

Mom sure does a great job with our yard. Just outside the door, I take a quick sniff and enjoy the cool morning air. Spread out before me is a wonderful mixture of colors, shapes and memories. In the summer months, pink and purple flowers are hung in baskets on the pillars that support our back patio cover. Just beyond the opening to the yard are two small boulders that act as a guide on the path up to a fire pit and stone seating. On a warmer day, I like to situate myself there and take in the sunshine. They say, "One, two, three strikes—you're out!" but I never am when I circle the pit three times each day for good measure. At night, we sometimes sit out here and just relax from the day. Out beyond the pit, the yard is sectioned off by a short concrete wall. Luckily, the wall is short enough—or maybe I am tall enough—that I can easily jump up and over it, onto the hill just behind, filled with beautiful and fragrant bushes and flowers. It seems like our yard goes on for miles, but a few more feet straight up leads to a fence that ties everything together.

Standing on the cement patio in my backyard, I scan the landscape and quickly discover my cotton-tailed furry friend has decided to move up on the hill. He appears to be checking out one of the bushes, and just my luck, is distracted. This is my opportunity to get a closer look. The little guy hasn't spotted me yet. I make a break for it and begin my quest.

Similar to a chess piece, I glide across the board that is my yard with pinpoint accuracy. I move from the patio out past some of Mom's planter boxes, and up a step to the fire pit. No worry of singeing my golden locks today, as the fire is turned off this time of year. Distracted for just a moment, I think about how fun it is to sit out here in the summer when the parentals make some sort of sandwich with crackers, chocolate, and gooey marshmallows. As the parentals are concerned about my health and well-being, any sample that comes my way doesn't include chocolate. It can be very bad for me to eat, but it sure does smell good. I also enjoy the heat from the fire, but for reasons I don't yet understand, my brother won't come anywhere close to the pit. I'm okay with that—more alone time with Mom and Dad for me.

The rabbit still hasn't spotted me; I've got skills. Today will be the day I finally catch up to him. Keep it together, Cockapoo. I leap over the small fire pit and approach the short concrete wall. I jump up and over, landing safely on the hill. From here, I can see back toward the house, as well as get a full view of the rest of the yard. In fact, when I need to get away and recharge, I like to come back here. This may be Mom and Dad's house and yard, but I'm really the queen of this here castle. Now, where is that rabbit?

Doo doo doo, nothing to see here. I begin a casual stroll across the top of the wall, minding my own business, but inching ever so closer to that hare. This is it; I'm going to run over and say hello and make a new frie— Just then, my so-called "bro," who has just discovered the rabbit, darts up the hill past me. My potential new friend looks startled and jumps to the corner of the fence by the post at the top of the hill, and with the brother-man bearing down, the rabbit slips under the fence and out of the yard. Grrr. Why can't Buddy play nice? To borrow a quote from my Mom's favorite movie, "He's a cotton-headed ninny muggins."

"Did you see that?" Buddy barks as he barrels down the hill, leaving nothing but mulch in his wake, all the while looking a little too proud of himself. "Pretty cool, huh?" Turning my head, I refuse to acknowledge his presence. As if on cue, Dad opens the sliding glass door, and we both bolt inside. Well, my potential new friend, until next time.

Once in the kitchen, I head directly to my bowl. While the brother-man spins around and around like a top, I patiently wait for the pending meal. Look at him, acting like a little child. He can't stand still. Drool starts to run from his mouth. Dad opens the container that houses the delectable delights and scoops food into each of our bowls, then sets them down on the floor by our water. I'm in business. I enjoy savoring my food, tasting each morsel. The nuances between the salmon and rice are pleasing to my palate. A nice balance to enjoy. I take a couple of bites. Yum, that's good stuff. Slowly, I go back for a little more. Kudos to Mom and Dad for selecting this particular assortment. My compliments to the chef.

By comparison, the "other one" has already finished. If I were to give him a name that best sums up his approach (if you want to call it that), it would be Hoover. I don't think he actually chews. No, he just inhales the food as fast as possible. All that's missing to make his transformation to a Hoover complete is the horrid sound from that weapon of death, the vacuum cleaner, as I hear it called. It is sort of mesmerizing to watch Buddy eat. Similar to a train wreck. You can't look away. What a disgusting display. Is he a hobbit? He does have hair on his feet. Does he think a second breakfast is on the way, so that he must eat the first one as fast as possible? Hmm, second breakfast; I could get behind that.

As he runs off, I finally have a minute to myself. Still enjoying my food, I take my time and once finished, move to the water bowl and quench my thirst. It's fresh; Dad must have put some water in here while we were outside. Nothing like the taste of cool, clear water to wash down a scrumptious meal.

What's this? In the middle of my water break, I see Dad out of the corner of my eye heading to the pantry. Pretending not to notice, I continue my hydration and see him pull a bag of bread out and head back to the counter. Bread. I do love me some bread. Perhaps second breakfast is an option after all. Walking over to Dad, I bark, "Hello," and ask, "What are you doing?" Dad puts two pieces of bread into the toaster and they start to heat up. Two pieces—he's so thoughtful. How did he know I would like a piece? I'll be sure to add him to my Christmas card list this year. I put my paws up on the counter to take in the smell of the bread as it's being toasted.

"Down, Sydney," he says. "This is my breakfast and isn't for you." Well, the nerve of some people. He's off the list.

Dad then heads back to the pantry area and comes back with…is that what I think it is? Peanut butter! Torture! This is sheer torture! Click, the toast pops up and Dad reaches for a knife from the top drawer, spreading the creamy peanut butter over the hot bread. Dad once told me he was born in the city where this smooth goodness is made. What a lucky guy. Peanut butter smells terrific once the top on the jar is opened, but it takes on a new level of aroma when added to toasted bread. Dad, you're killing me here. Can I please have some? I paw his leg to let him know I mean business. Dad turns, looks to make sure my brother isn't around—or for that matter, Mom— and scoops a little on a spoon, bending down to let me have a taste. So rich, so heavenly, so delicious. That's what I'm talking about! The peanut butter sticks to the woof of my mouth, I mean roof, but I don't care as I lick it up. It tastes so good. After every last tidbit is consumed, Dad looks at the spoon and notes that he won't even need to wash it, as I did such a good job cleaning it.

"Yes, you will!" I hear Mom exclaim, walking back into the kitchen. Busted.

"Okay, Sydney, that's all I have for you." Dad takes his toast over to the table to sit and eat his meal. I follow and sit right next to him. I look up at him lovingly. I am very attentive and perhaps the best friend he could ask for. I gently paw at his leg, telling him telepathically, "I can surely help you finish that if you can't handle it all." He continues to eat. Hmm, perhaps he didn't feel the loving gesture.

"Eh, um," I bark, "still here and happy to help in any way I can." One piece down, he starts on the second, and yes, final piece. Time to get serious. I circle the table and head to his other side. Bite after excruciating bite, I watch the last piece of toast slowly disappear. Just to be clear, yes, I did already eat. Yes, I had some water, and yes, I enjoyed the taste of peanut butter. But have I had any toast? No! Do I want some toast? Is that even a question? Dad turns to me. Finally, toast is headed my way.

"Sydney, this is wheat bread."

I turn my head to one side. "I'm sorry, your point here?"

"You're allergic to wheat and can't have any. Sorry."

So, I'm allergic to wheat? I'm willing to take the risk if they are! I have one little issue with a wheat product and suddenly, I'm banned for life. "Not fair!" I protest.

"You heard your dad," Mom chimes in. "You don't want to go back to the V-E-T, do you?" Um, I can spell, thank you very much. I'm not a child. And no, I don't want that. Nobody wants that. Darn these food allergies. Foiled again.

CHAPTER 3
SYDNEY

GO GET IT! With a quick squeak, the yellow tennis ball flies through the air. It bounces several times down on the hardwood floor in the entryway of the house filled with bright sunshine on this autumn morning. Now that breakfast is over, it's time to play. As I am the master of the house, and self-described princess of the Snoqualmie Valley, I decide when it's time to play and the toy I will play with. Ready? Time to begin. I dart down the hallway after the object of my desire. Oh squeaky ball, how I love chasing after you. On this fall day, yours truly, Sydney Minich, I am in my element. Retrieving the orb, I trot back to my dad—I mean *past* my dad, actually—jumping up and land safely behind him on the couch. What can I say, I'm in a playful mood. My dad is silly; he thinks I'm going to bring the ball back to him. Ha! I'm of my own free will, and come and go as I please.

My dad removes the ball from my mouth, and with a quick double tap of the toy, back in the air it goes. I leap off the couch and prepare to race down the hall yet again. However, this time the ball is diverted from its flight plan and intercepted in mid-air by the less intelligent canine being, Buddy, or the one I occasionally call "Huff and Puff." I have many names for my brother, but this one applies because of all the panting he does.

Huff and Puff snatches the ball away and zooms back down the hall. I rue the day this interloper came to the house. I thought he was only staying for a visit. That visit has turned into years. I was the lone dog in the house for the first few years of my life until along came this shedding, smelly, clingy, and frankly, rude foe to my domain. Known to my parentals as my brother, I prefer the title of "arch nemesis." Gone are the days of lounging on the recliner chair with Dad, or quiet car rides with my nose out the window taking in all the wonderful smells, seeing little people walking back and forth all wanting to wave and say hello. No, the "Bud-man," as they call him—seriously, how many different names does he need—is always crowding me on Dad's chair, vying for space. And he talks incessantly in the car, yapping on and on out the window at my potential new friends. Well, on this morning, with *my* ball, I am not going to stand for it.

Buddy trots back to the middle of the room, ball still in his mouth, and lays down on the floor to play.

"Give it back," I say to him. "Give it back." To Mom and Dad, it sounds like we just sit and bark at each other. But Buddy and I can understand each other just fine, just as we understand all dogs. As if speaking was just for the parentals and humans only. Right!

Oblivious to my comments, he continues to play with his newfound treasure—my treasure. I run up to Dad. "He took my toy," I protest as I make my case. "Make him give it back! Doesn't he understand the tennis ball is my personal property and he has no right to take it from me?"

Dad gets up, walks over to the one who shall not be named, and removes the ball from his mouth. Dad holds it up in the air and I scamper over. "Yes, that is mine, please give it to me."

Quickly the ball is flung back down the hall. I love giving chase. The two of us race for the toy. Lighter and faster on my feet, I outpace my rival. Reaching the ball first, I quickly pick it up and turn to my left, as my brother attempts to swipe it from my mouth with his paw and steal it from me. Too bad, so sad. I thwart his plan with a little duck and cover and begin to prance back down the hall toward my dad, when out of nowhere, Huff and Puff bumps into me. In that moment, the ball drops out of my mouth. Before I can react, Buddy swoops in and snags the ball away and rushes back to the middle of the room. So not cool.

Refusing to look at my brother, I trot right back up to dad again. "I feel like I'm stating the obvious here, but he took my ball again, and as you can clearly see, won't give it back." The nerve!

My dad stands in the room and just stares at me. What, doesn't he understand what I just said? Finally, he points to where we keep all of our toys. "How about another one?"

"What? No, I don't want any of those other silly toys. No, I'm taking a stand. I want the toy that was taken from me." I tap my paw on the floor and bark, "No." My dad attempts to help and remove my ball from, well, you know who. This time, though, Buddy doesn't want to give the ball back. Who does the think he is? Why, he's acting like a common terrier.

Buddy says, "Mine, mine, mine!" Backing off, dad offers me another ball, which he squeaks and tosses in the other direction. Is he kidding? I will not be distracted with some other dog toy.

"Well," my dad says, "your brother is playing with the toy. If you want it, you need to ask him to share." Dad puts his hands up in the air as he heads to the kitchen.

Oh, no, he didn't! Share. The wheels have really come off the bus this time. Okay, enough playing games. I walk back to the other one and demand my toy be returned. I tell him, "You already ruined my day once with the rabbit—I will not have this happen again." I repeat this multiple times. Buddy stares directly at me and his eyes don't even blink. Can Buddy not hear? Is he not paying attention to me? I move in front of him, crouch really low, get in his grill and ask one last time for my ball. I will not ask again. Buddy pulls the ball under his paw and only offers up a quick "no." I lose it and pin him like those wrestlers my dad watches on the "pane of knowledge" when my mom isn't home. Didn't see that one coming, did you, Bud? We tussle for a moment, rolling across the floor and bouncing off one of the couches. In the skirmish, dad instructs us to stop horsing around. Whatever, like we're animals or something?

Stopping for a quick breath, we continue our sibling struggle for control. In all the confusion with pillows now flying, my dad comes over to break up the fight. The ball drops to the floor and I make my move. Yes, got it! Before Huff and Puff realizes what's going on, I vacate the room, my prized squeaky ball in my mouth, and head upstairs. Take my ball, will you? I think not.

CHAPTER 4

BUDDY

DUDE! MY SISTER WAS JUST HERE a minute ago and now she's gone. Trippy! Did I imagine that? Am I talking to myself? Can myself hear me? Hello self!

"Hello." Yikes!

Hey, I'm getting pretty good at conversating. I could be onto something here. It feels like my head is resting nicely on a giant puffy pillow.

"Buddy," I hear my dad say. "Don't worry too much about your sister. She can be a little grumpy in the morning."

My Pops is very smart. I always listen to my Pops.

"Buddy," I hear him say again. "Are you just going to lay there with the pillow on the floor in defeat or are you going to play with another ball?"

So wise. Wait, did he say another ball? I do love playing with squeaky toy balls. Hmm, where did they all go? Turning to the left, don't see any, to the right, nope!

"Um, Buddy. You look lost. If you're looking for more toys they're on the dog bed... behind you."

Turning around, I see many toys to play with. How does Pops do that? Blue ones, orange ones, and ooh red. I like red. I snatch the toy up and dart over and jump up on the couch. Chomping on the toy, squeak! Yes, I love that sound.

"Have fun, Bud," I hear Pops say as he leaves the room.

The only thing more fun would be a nap. Ooh, naps, I love naps.

CHAPTER 5
SYDNEY

I BREEZE UP THE STAIRS and notice Buddy isn't giving chase. That's the smartest thing he's done all day. I sit for a minute and catch my breath. Maybe I should lay off some of the extra peanut butter. Glancing down the stairs, I confirm he didn't follow and head to the guest room, a.k.a. the Pepsi room. This is one of my favorite rooms in the house. It brings together the parentals's shared love of the caffeinated beverage. Even if they're aren't home, it reminds me of them. Red and blue Pepsi tin signs decorate the bedroom walls. On the lone antique dresser, the motif continues with a red and blue die-cast Pepsi delivery truck—Diet Pepsi, mind you. There's a Pepsi piggy bank disguised as a vending machine and a miniature six pack containing that special blend of sugar and caffeine Dad enjoys. The bed is adorned with a matching throw and pillow tying together a more vintage feel for the room.

Time to go to work. I have a very short commute, just like my mom. We both work from home. Normally, Dad would be off to work himself, but I overheard them talking and he's working here today, too. I jump onto the bed with the world's fastest flying start. When I land, I feel the fine stitching and wonderfully soft texture of the Amish quilt Mom and Dad brought back from the family road trip a few years ago to the "Crossroads of America" as Dad calls it—Indiana to everyone else. Bad memories start to surface. Too many days trapped in a car with…him. The brother. That smell. If you rolled around in the dirt, sat in the hot sun all day and walked for three miles, you would come somewhere close to that odor. Oh dear! He always carries the smell with him, but the close quarters inside a motorized vehicle are often times too much. Honestly, has he heard of cleaning himself from time to time? Don't get me started; that's a story for a different day. Right now, it's time to set up shop for the day.

I walk across the surface of the quilt and come upon the perfectly arranged and overstuffed pillows that will act as my desk for the day. If I'm to get my important work done, this setup simply won't do. I burrow through the first layer of pillows to situate my body between the next two queen-size pillows. Ah, now that's better. I'm now in the perfect position to view my "monitor" for the day. At this vantage point, perched in the upstairs bedroom, I can see out of the window in the front of our house, which affords me a great view of the whole neighborhood. If anyone comes up or down the street, I am aware of it and take note.

Looking straight ahead at my "screen," I follow the black driveway that leads up a slight incline into wooded brush. From up on high, I can see any number of potential new friends, or even bears who might be crossing, as noted on a yellow sign out front of our neighbor's house. The deer should be out soon for their morning feeding. If I'm lucky, maybe I'll catch another glimpse of my furry friend from the backyard who hops in and out from time to time. Turning just to my left, I can see what Mom and Dad refer to as the cul-de-sac. Interesting, this layout. I love the circular design, but don't understand why you only go around once. I always circle in threes. Once for observation. Twice for escape routes in case of emergency. Third, and this is my favorite, because I march to the beat of my own drum. Dare to be different, I say. Vehicles travel up the street in one direction, and this road course directs them around in a circle and sends them back from where they came.

Periodically, I spot a big box on wheels that will stop in front of the house; sometimes, a human will emerge from said box, walk to our front door and ring the doorbell. Oh, how I love it when the bell rings. Music to my ears. That ding dong means someone new is here. A potential friend. I can be anywhere in the house and when that tone hits my ears, it's organized chaos as I leap into action to greet a new guest.

I love my job. I work hard each and every day keeping these mean streets safe from harm. Well, I do what I can. Nothing gets past me, for I am on watch. Neighborhood watch. Proceed with caution; you've been notified.

Since I was so rudely and prematurely awakened this morning, I am still sleepy, and I need to shake the cobwebs loose. Mom and Dad will work for hours on end staring into their own monitors. I do enjoy the view from here, but hours on end? I consider a nap, but suddenly I see movement at 10 o'clock. The silver paint shines off the window, alerting me to this potential intruder. Advancing on one of those two wheeled cycles, someone is sure peddling hard down the street. Perhaps they are lost and will circle around and head the other…Wait, we have a security breach. The cyclist exits the street and begins the slight incline on the drive directly in front of my house. My tail begins to wag. Keep it together, focus on your training. "Hey, there," I bark. "You there on the cycle, I can see you. You don't have the right credentials to be on the drive." The cyclist stops in his tracks.

In this opportune moment, I get a good look at the threat. Dark blue knit hat pulled down almost over his eyes with stringy hair running down to his neck. No wonder he entered the neutral zone. He obviously can't see. His clothes don't seem to match and he's got on two different types of shoes. Not just colors, shoes. What appears to be a tennis shoe on one foot and a flip flop on the other. This guy doesn't have a clue. Over his shoulder is some sort of bag that seems a little bulky. Are these his school supplies? Reaching into the bag, he pulls out what appears to be paper of some sort held together by a rubber band. He climbs off his two-wheeled vehicle and steps onto the driveway, my driveway.

Code Blue! I begin to bark again, giving him a little more growl this time to show I'm serious. The interloper continues toward the house and I tap the window with my paw and move my body as close to the monitor as I can. "You're not cleared to be this close to the house. Halt or I will have to alert the parentals." He seems startled and stops in his tracks. Looking up at the window, our eyes meet for the first time. "That's right, you're busted." I give him my best snarl and he tosses the paper toward the house, but doesn't advance any further. Retreating to his ride, he hops on and spins around heading back off the grid. Guess he know not to mess with this hound. Well, I'm awake and alert now. Okay, who's next? Just be careful, I've got my eye on you.

CHAPTER 6

SYDNEY

ON THIS CRISP FALL MORNING, the orange and yellow leaves continue their descent, covering the streets in my quiet little town. I've been busy watching the little ones in the 'hood as they emerge from their homes with their backpacks in tow. They are off to what will be another exciting day of knowledge building. The older versions, the rebellious ones, what with their oversized pants, sideways caps and white buds in their ears with mysterious wires dangling to parts unknown, don't have to walk to school like the little ones do. No, they have their own vehicles and either drive themselves or have other hooligans drive over and pick them up. Apparently, they are too cool for this thing the parentals call school. This is a typical morning for this time of year. The weather has changed and the youngsters are back on a more formal schedule.

Diagonal from my vantage point, I see a garage door slowly begin to open. Yay, my three favorite ladies, outside of my mom, are getting ready to head out for the day. First, I can see one of my mom's besties, River, as she works to bring one of the waste receptacles to the curb. She has short straight blonde hair and always has a smile on her face. I love her. She gives me hugs. River is the mom to the two other smaller ones who live with her, one of whom—the oldest daughter, Fitz—is now emerging from the garage. Looks like she's got on her pink backpack ready for the day as she stops for a second to tie one of her shoes. Pink is one of my favorite colors. I love Fitz. She gives me kisses.

She calls to her sister, and I now see Palmer trailing behind. She is the youngest and similar in height to me. Okay, she's shorter than her sibling and lower to the ground like me, and always has coloring pencils and paper with her and when she comes over for a visit. We sit and draw together. I love her. She gives me hugs and kisses. Both girls have hair of gold, like their mother. Palmer's is starting to curl. River hugs both girls as they walk down the street toward the bus stop where the big orange box will take them to school. Uh oh; it looks like something just fell out of Palmer's bag. I try to notify her from my perch in my house but they don't stop and must be unable to hear me. I hope I get to see them and go for a walk together later this afternoon. I do love the outdoors and exploration and I know where I want to go first today — to see what fell out of her bag.

Quiet begins to set in; the morning rush must be over. I let out a big yawn. All of this attention to everyone else's detail can be tiring and take a lot out of a cockapoo. As the garage door closes at River's house, I see her starting to walk toward our place.

Just at that moment, Mom walks in my office and asks me another of my all-time favorite questions. "Sydney," she says, "Do you want to go for a ride?" Are squeaky balls round? Of course I want to go for a ride. My tail is already wagging.

Mom tells me that River has called and is on her way over, and since I've been so good this morning, she thought I might enjoy a little trip. Mom so gets me.

Mom and River often go to this place called a gym to do this thing called working out. It also seems to be a social thing where many ladies come to chat, and I do love to gab. I immediately jump off the bed and sprint downstairs with lightning speed, reaching the bottom step in mere seconds. I hear Mom tell Dad she is off to the gym. She quickly opens the door leading to the garage, and out we go before Buddy (who now seems to be asleep on the couch) can figure out what's going on. Once in the garage, Mom opens the door and as it continues to move up and up. I can now see River standing in the driveway. Hugs, right on cue. Mom then escorts me over to her vehicle and I jump in. With River on board, Mom backs out and we're off. Look out, world.

Since I'm on the subject of vehicles, and am now riding in one, I should mention that I don't yet have one of my own. Most of the time I ride in my Mom's all-wheel drive, like today, or SUV, as I've heard them called. It has lots of room and apparently seats five full-size humans. When we do head out as a family unit, I'm not crowded by my foe—oh, whoops, I mean bro. You can see how I would get that confused. The space in the back-seat allows me to stretch out and not be crowded by a certain someone. To keep us safe, Mom and Dad have harnesses they strap onto us that lock into the clicker holding the belt in place. I understand the need to be safe, but I also like to explore and this contraption limits my movements. Oh, well, take the good, take the bad, I guess. Hey, that could almost be a song.

In Mom's car, I sit in the backseat and I'm perched up high and can see activity coming and going from various vantage points. The SUV has a cover over the seats, apparently to keep it clean from my brother's and my paws. Um, I clean them every day so I don't know what the deal is, but whatever. The parentals also insist on using some sort of spray that's supposed to smell like a breeze. I've heard this is done because, and I quote here, "the vehicle smells like dog." Does my brother have a special funk about him? Yes. Should I be lumped in with that special funk? I think not. What Mom really means is the ride smells like Buddy.

If I'm really good, I sometimes get to ride in Dad's vehicle. His ride is quite different. Dad's ride is very low to the ground. His vehicle doesn't have a back seat and has only two doors. I've heard the term "sports car" tossed around when they are talking about it. Dad just calls it his dream car. It doesn't take much for me to get inside. Just a quick jump; I don't even break a sweat. The soft seating surface smells really good, but is slick, and I always tend to slide around before finding my grip. Where Mom's SUV makes a higher pitched noise when starting, Dad's is more of a roar. His vehicle rumbles in a throaty, "Don't-mess-with-me" kind of way. In a word, awesome! His car also incorporates something called shifting, where Mom's seems more automatic to me. Sometimes when my brother and I are out with Mom, we will meet up with Dad along the way. Using my cunning skills—because, yes, I'm crafty—I can persuade Dad to get a ride home with him. Where Mom is a more conservative driver, Dad prefers to move quicker. The seats really hug me when we go around corners in his ride. His vehicle also has some getup, and we have no trouble getting from place to place in no time flat.

I remember there was this one time Dad met all of us for dinner. Why must I always stay in the car while they dine out? Sure, they always check to make sure the temperature is not too hot in the car, but dogs need food as well. I need to talk to them about that. After their meal, the parentals came back to greet my brother and me. "Syd," Dad said to me, "why don't you come ride with me?"

Ride with you, and without my brother? Where do I sign? I was squirming so much Dad had trouble unhooking me from the harness. Once free, Dad picked me up and set me on the concrete. Attached to my leash, I practically pulled him over to his car. Dad opened the door and I jumped inside. Locking me back in via the harness, Dad fired up the car and we followed

Mom home. Well, I thought we were following her home. Mom went one direction while Dad went an alternate route. Having ridden with him before, I could tell something was up. Dad likes to be adventurous. It became apparent very quickly Dad was not taking the normal route home. The pace of the car picked up and the soft seats really held me in place as we zipped down some less traveled streets.

"Syd," Dad said to me, "don't worry, I just wanted to try a different way home." Truth be told, that's why I'm here. I think Dad wanted to get home first. Perhaps this was some sort of challenge. As we continued on, I was very excited, listening to the hum of the engine, occasional squeal of the tires around corners and feeling the acceleration of the ride. At the same time, I became concerned. Just where was Dad going? On past trips, he'd gotten lost before. I'm not supposed to mention that, but seeing as how this is my flashback, he shouldn't mind.

During the ride, the sun went down and Dad turned on the headlights. This was no mere set of lights that came on and provided guidance for our way home. No, this was a cool process. Dad turned a knob next to his steering wheel and I could hear a whooshing sound coming from the engine area. Suddenly, the lights flipped up from their hiding place under the hood. He's done this before and it never gets old. I felt like one of those super beings who have a special auto they ride in to fight crime. All I was missing was a cape.

The light cut through the darkness and it felt like we had been in the car awhile. If he was trying to get home first, I don't think he was succeeding. Just then, Dad made a quick right hand turn and our speed really picked up. I mean, push-you-back-in-your-seat picked up. Wait, this place looked familiar. I'd been on this road before. How did he do that? The concern for being lost was now transformed to a thrill.

Up in the distance, I could see what looked like the back end of my Mom's ride. Dad used the knob next to the steering wheel to identify his direction and changed position on the road. Just like that, we pulled up alongside Mom's ride. I turned, and with a tick tack, I put my paws on the window. I could see Mom, who quickly gave me a wave. Then Dad matched the speed of her car. I could see my brother in the back seat. It took him a good five seconds before he realized I was staring at him. Dad honked his horn and we started to pull past them. I gave my brother a quick wave and we were off. Dad did make it home first, but when we got to our street that night he stopped to wave my mom on by. In all the excitement, I had forgotten how good the inside of Dad's ride smelled. As we followed Mom up the street I was able to sit back and take in the intoxicating smell. A special blend of apples and pumpkin with just a dash of mechanical parts thrown in for good measure. Sniff, sniff.

All this daydreaming of vehicles has made me lose track of time, and Mom now pulls into the parking lot of the gym. The morning is just flying by.

"Okay, Syd," she says. "Stay here, and River and I will be back in a bit."

Before exiting the vehicle, Mom rolls down the windows, allowing for a cool breeze to cross over my fur. I love Mom. She always looks out for me. Today is cool and with the combination of airflow I'm quite comfortable in the car. She would never leave me or my brother in the car on a warmer day unattended. No worries, Mom. I'm on patrol.

CHAPTER 7

BUDDY

WOOF, WOOF, I HEAR SOMETHING. I have good ears. What do I hear? Not sure, but I will bark at it one more time just to make sure. Woof! Sitting on the couch, my Pops walks over toward me and gives me a soft pet on my head.

"Your mom and sister have gone out, Bud. Just you and me."

Sweet, I love bro time. Pops sits next to me and gazes at this rectangle object, ooh rectangle, with what look like an apple with a piece missing on the back. Ooh, apple. He continues to pet me as I calm down from the noise I heard. Sitting together, I begin to clean my paws. I like to clean. I lick my paws, the couch, Dad's pants. I even try to lick the fruit on the rectangle but Dad indicates that's a bit much. If you need a cleaning, I'm your bud. Hey, that's my name! Dad gets up and heads to the kitchen. Since he's not looking, I start to lick the rectangle anyway. Hmm, this doesn't taste like an apple.

"Buddy, what are you doing over there, dude?" asks Pops. "Stop licking the tablet. The action is over here. Got a surprise for you." Oh boy, oh boy, I do love surprises. They are like my favoritest thing ever, until I discover something else and then that becomes my favorite. Shah, like I don't store a lot in the noggin, you know. Helps me keep my focus and stay fresh when important things come up, like this. Don't want all that other stuff getting in the way, like these thoughts and ideas I keep hearing about. Whoa, need a moment. Thoughts racing at me all at once. Okay, calm down, dude. Hit the reset button. Remember your drills. Step one, focus, step two... well, I got at least one step today. Progress.

"Bud-man, where are you?" Totally, I am going to go in the kitchen to hang with my Pops. Traction, trying to gain traction on the slippery floor made of wood. One and two and three—uh oh! Too much speed. Stop, need to stop. How do I get off this crazy ride? Brakes, time to apply the brakes. Wall, kitchen wall. I'm about to crash into the kitchen wall. Yikes, that was scary. Close, but

I missed the full impact this time. Excellent. Here I am! Here I am!

Running up to my Pops, I quickly show him some love. Hugs and kisses, hugs and kisses. I almost climb up his leg, I'm so excited to see him again. Hugs and kisses. It's like I haven't seen him in however long you would judge time and stuff. Sis would call it minutes or something. To be honest, I'm not so good with calculations.

"Okay, Buddy, now sit," says my Pop. I plop my butt right on the ground. I may not remember many things at one time, but I'm good at following commands when dished out in samples. Yum, samples. Dad opens his hand and I can see what appears to be the tasty crunchy snacks filled with miniature peanut butter squares, also known as nuggets. These are Dad's special treats. Nugget. My head hurts from that one. Do I get extra credit for such a big-time word?

"Now, Buddy," Pops continues. "Sydney can't have these because they contain wheat, but she's out of the house right now and what she doesn't know won't hurt her, right?" Radical! Nodding my head, I agree with him a million times, yes. Holding the treat over my head, he instructs me to stay. Roger, staying put. You're not going to see this guy move. Pops then tosses the treat up in the air. Watching it spin, as if in slow motion, I jump up from the wood floor and catch the sucker in mid-air.

"Nice job," Pops says. Of course, I think to myself, I come spring loaded. "Okay, Bud, how about a couple more before your sister comes in?" Pops repeats the move three more times and the floor has never looked so clean. Not one morsel has hit the ground. Ooh, morsel, wonder if Pops has any more? I see him dig into the container and toss a couple in his mouth, and then head to the front room of the house. Cool, he digs peanut butter too. Like the good and obedient boy that I am, I quickly follow. Dad finishes the nuggets but gives me one last bite. As he sits down to "start work" as he calls it, I stay right next to him and wallow around on the floor like the crazy hound that I am. Carpet feels good today.

CHAPTER 8
SYDNEY

ABOUT AN HOUR LATER, I find myself saying goodbye to River as Mom and I head back into the house. It is now toward the end of my morning work session. Time to take a break from the heavy stress of my work day. Once upstairs, I quickly make my way down the carpeted hallway into the bedroom for a catnap. Hey, dogs nap, too, you know. How did cats get ahold of that word anyway? I'll have to get on that later; there are more pressing things to cover right now. I enter the bedroom and hear Mom and Dad as they meet at the top of the stairs talking about plans for dinner later today. I have just enough time to get some rest before I have to go back down to grace them with my presence.

I climb up onto my ultra-soft double-decker bed. Some time ago, the parentals bought new beds for me and my brother and decided to place the new installments directly on top of the older models. The original dog beds were of a square nature and all of the stuffing got pushed out to the edges. The new beds are circular and Dad positioned them right on top. I don't know how he did it, but this allows me to be centered with a cushion on the cloud of fluff from the new bed and yet be supported by the old. He's so cool. I circle three times and make sure to find just the right spot to rest my weary head. As I drift off, a wonderful aroma enters my nose. Mom is starting lunch already; it smells so good. Pleasant dreams.

With a sudden thud, I wake up from my dream. Taking a quick look around, I don't see anything out of place. Was that live or Memorex? Well, this is a good time to sit up and stretch out. I leave my hind quarters on the bed and stretch my front paws out in front of me as far as they can go. Ah, that feels good. Sniff, sniff. I smell the lunch Mom has been making during my nap. The heavenly scent wafts through the bedroom from the kitchen downstairs. In my mind, I can practically hear the sizzle of bubbling cheese frying on the hot sandwich thingy. Sniff, sniff. Do I smell smoked turkey, with a dash of barbeque sauce? She must have made her world famous grilled goodness. Sometimes, Mom lets me try whatever she is making. I'm a lucky cock-apoo and have tried lots of food like turkey, roast beef, hot dogs, carrots, apples, peanut butter... I could go on and on. Having tried turkey before, I can only imagine how good it will taste smoked. I do love lunch—or any meal for that matter.

Boy oh boy, will they be excited to see me. Now that I am so refreshed and renewed, Mom and Dad won't be able to resist my charms and surely will let me have some of that delicious smelling treat. "Hold up, I'm coming."

Wait a minute. Why is the bedroom door closed? A chill comes over my whole body and stops me dead in my tracks. I bolt up to the door and crouch down really low. Carefully, I take a look through the crack under the door. I feel a gentle breeze from the air conditioning that must have come on recently. Uh oh, gentle breeze. Oh no. This particular bedroom door tends to have a mind of its own and sometimes closes all by itself. Through deductive reasoning, thoughtful analysis and overhearing Mom and Dad talk about it, I know that the door tends to close when the A/C or heat comes on and the subsequent airflow created pulls the door shut. The thud I heard in my dream must have been the door closing.

Okay, nothing to be concerned about here. I will just let Mom and Dad know I'm awake and ready for quality time, a.k.a. Sydney time. "Hello," I bark. "Hello!" I repeat this again and again. After a minute of identifying my desire to join the rest of the group, I stop and listen. No one is coming. I again crouch really low by the door. I can now hear sounds of grown men grunting. A whistle blows in the background, and I hear the now familiar tone of sportscaster Al Michaels. Mom and Dad must be watching one of these events on the pane of knowledge where grown men put on padding and chase after a pigskin ball. I know this because my brother and I have been known to sit and watch. When the Seattle Seahawks, our local team, score, my brother and I cheer, as this seems to please the parentals. Right now I have more pressing matters to deal with. The odd part of this noise from downstairs is I don't hear Mom's and Dad's voices. "Hello," I bark again. I start to scratch the door now. Can't they hear me? "Hello!" If I were only taller and had thumbs, this wouldn't be an issue.

Sniff, sniff. I smell the savory aroma of my all-time favorite cheese, cheddar. I love it so much; I even traveled to the factory once with Mom and Dad where they make this orange delight. Did I get to go in? No. Do I still have an issue with this? Yes. The fragrance from downstairs, coming up through the open floor vents, is consuming the room. Cruel and unusual punishment indeed. Trouble. Putting two and two together, I realize Mom and Dad don't know I'm trapped in here. Worse yet, where did they go? They don't appear to be in the house. "Hello!" I shout again. "I'm in here!"

No response. Nothing but the sounds coming from the game. I'm so hungry now. I didn't even have a snack earlier. The horror. To make matters worse, as if that's even possible, I now have to use the facility. I walk back to the middle of the room thinking, what do I do? Think, Cockapoo, think! Then my mind focuses on one single thing—voices from outside. I hear voices coming from the front side of the house. How did I not notice it before? I run to the window and without hesitation nudge the shade covering the cool glass out of the way with my nose. Mom and Dad are in front of the house talking to other humans.

With a slap, the shade bumps into the back of my head and pushes my face into the cool glass. How rude. Poking my nose through again, I also see the "other one" outside with them. "Hello, hello! I'm up here. I'm hungry and if you don't hurry, we may have another set of issues." The Bud-man glances in my direction. Making eye contact, I bark to him, "I'm up here! The door is closed and I need some assistance. Please instruct Mom or Dad to come upstairs and let me out." What? Did he just smile at me and then do nothing? He turns around and faces the neighbors, and begins saying hello to them instead. Words fail me. Why, the many times I've helped him out of a… Never mind. Okay, so I may deserve a little of this payback. I will deal with him later. Assuming I ever make it out of here.

I hear Mom say, "Okay, see you next week," and with a thud, the front door closes. The elders are back inside. Darting back to the bedroom door, I frantically scratch the wood on the underside of the door and let out a little whimper. "Here! I'm up here!" I say. I can hear Mom and Dad talking. "Help! I need help!" Dropping to the floor, I try pushing my paws underneath the door to make some noise. Wait. Are those footsteps on the stairs? I hear the distinct sound of Dad's walk. He likes his footwear. Dad owns the same brand of shoe in many colors and fabrics. I can hear his shoe laces hitting the rubber section that covers the toe area as he walks. Almost like the start of a song. One, two, one two three four. Hey, I'm a dog, it's my job to notice subtleties like this. Those Chuck Taylors have never sounded so good. I feel the vibration of someone approaching the room now and smell the familiar odor of Dad's cologne. TGIF. My tail seems to have a mind of its own and is wagging uncontrollably at this point.

Finally, the door opens and I hear Dad say, "Sydney, I didn't know you were in here." Didn't know, I thought. Well, not time for that now. Almost spinning Dad around, I zip past him and make it to the top of the stairs, dig my claws into the plush carpet to make the sharp turn around the corner, and then down the stairs I go. Dad calls from behind, "I think Sydney got locked in the bedroom." I land on the hardwood floor downstairs, and see Mom heading to the back door as she asks if I want to take a break. Um, yeah. On a mission here, people. I don't stop to say hello, pass go, or even collect my two hundred dollars. Rude, I know. I fly past Mom and out the back door.

CHAPTER 9

SYDNEY

RETURNING FROM MY BREAK, I enter the kitchen through the sliding glass door, and instantly my nose fills with a melting pot of scents, all competing for my attention. A strong pumpkin pie smell is coming from the high bar counter, conveniently out of reach. Whatever! Next, the smell of fresh chocolate chip cookies leads me over to the entry way with a delicious scent just above my line of sight. And, is that the intoxicating scent of banana bread coming from the bathroom? Indeed it is. Even though I don't eat desserts, a girl can dream about them. Wait, I smell what's happening here. Mom has cleverly used these smells to distract me. Why it's, it's several of those pillars of light Mom likes to bring home from the store. I think she calls them "candles," made by some Yankee. Normally, this would have worked on my brother, but I'm on to her. I smelled cheese earlier. She's got real food somewhere. Time to lay on the charm and score some lunch. Mom is pretty smart, but no match for this four-legged wonder.

Ordinarily, getting lunch snacks wouldn't be a problem. The parentals are often outwitted by my longing gaze, gentle paw caresses on their arms, and my stunt performing abilities for their amusement when it comes to securing some good time treats. But no! There must be some trickery here, I tell you. Strange things are afoot at the Circle K. The food items are nowhere to be found. I survey my territory again, but see nothing. Did I miss something? Mom is upstairs. Dad has gone back to the dining room. My brother appears to have vanished into thin air. Am I in the right house? Finally, I hear footsteps coming from Dad's general direction. Answers, I need some answers.

"You look lost," Dad says to me, entering the kitchen. "Can I help you with something?"

"Cheese!" I bark. "I smelled cheese earlier and was briefly distracted by these candles."

"Syd, you're going to have to give me a little more detail. I'm not sure what you need."

"Lunch," I bark. I walk over to the kitchen counter and put my front paws up to look around. I know food was here.

"Syd, off!" Sliding slowly back the ground, I am stumped. I put my head down. What happened? I've lost my mojo.

"Wait," Dad says to me. "You're looking for food, aren't you? I'm sorry, but you're a few minutes too late. We already ate."

Wha-, what! It's like I just lost as a contestant on the show where the price might be right.

"Syd," he continues. "You ate this morning, remember? Don't worry, if you're a good girl you can have a treat a little later."

"I am so not cool with this," I bark.

"Hey," Dad says. "I have last night's game on the DVR. What do you say we both sit down, take a little rest and watch? Your mom is upstairs on a conference call; it would be just you and me for a bit. I'm still on my lunch break and my next meeting isn't for a half hour."

I do love sitting with Dad and cozying up to him while we watch the pane of knowledge. "Okay," I bark.

"Ready, break," Dad says to me. He needs to get out more.

I beat Dad over to the recliner and eagerly wait for him to arrive. Remind myself never to get old.

"Come on, Dad," I bark, "You only have 30 minutes." Finally he arrives and sits in the chair. In one long sweeping motion, he reaches for the handle on the side of the chair and pushes his body backwards as the bottom foot rest rises, allowing for a nice smooth surface for me to jump up and sit between his two legs. He positions the chair a bit with the inner workings, making some noise as he does so. Quality time with your dad, a girl can get used to this.

Dad pets me on the head for a few seconds before I turn around to watch the game with him. Peaceful, calm, all is right with the world. Just settled, I hear a noise from the second floor. My brother comes thundering down the stairs. Wham. I think he just hit the wall at the bottom. It never ceases to amaze me. He travels up and down those stairs multiple times a day and can't seem to brake in time. Silly boy dog. Quiet times may be ending earlier than I hoped.

I barely have time to raise my head before Buddy collects himself and runs over towards Dad's chair. "There you are, Bud," Dad says, and that's all it takes for Buddy to leap right at us and land directly on top of me. How do I get this two ton heavy thing off of me? "Help," I bark. It's like I've just taken a bath outside in the mud and it has instantly dried on me. How he doesn't notice this on a daily basis I'll never know.

"Give your sister some space there, Bud," Dad says. Buddy, always the listener, doesn't move and instead contorts his body so he can start kissing Dad on the face. I growl a little bit at Buddy to have him move. Instead, he just continues to lick Dad. Must he lick everything in sight? Wait, this is Buddy, so yes. Dad moves Buddy back a bit and guides him to the foot rest portion of the chair while I snuggle up closer to Dad's thigh. This lasts for one, two seconds at most, as Buddy can't stand to be that far away from Dad. He loves attention more than me. Perhaps craves is a better word.

Here he comes again back toward Dad. "No," I growl at him. "This is my time with Dad. Don't test me. You've been down that road once today, mister." I apply an extra grrr, and Buddy stops for a second. I put my head back down on the chair and try to look past him toward the game. Five seconds go by, and just when I think he's headed my way, he rearranges himself on the chair. He puts his head down and turns away from me. He's got some spunk, I'll give him that, but there's only so much I can handle. I believe he's now discovered how much. At least I'm no longer getting a sample of the aroma from Tacoma. Finally, there it is, quiet time with my Dad. Well, almost.

CHAPTER 10
SYDNEY

DAD PETS ME ON MY HEAD. "Hey, Syd. Time for me to go back to work." Buddy and I jump off the chair and Dad heads down the hallway toward the front of the house, my brother in tow. Time for me to get back as well. I zip upstairs and go back to my post. I'm still on the clock after all, and with the shenanigans of the last hour or so, I need to get back on my watch. Plenty of things keeping me busy today. Hearing a rickety racket sound coming from down the street, my focus becomes razor sharp yet again. Mom and Dad are lucky to have me on patrol.

A big pick-'em up truck is rolling my direction, pulling a trailing object that appears to hold a muncher of grass, giant clippers and long sticks with spades attached to them, also known as yard equipment. The convoy stops near the front of our house. I've discovered that my Dad does not enjoy this yard work thing. If Mom goes outside to water plants, trim some bushes or plant new flowers, Dad seems to mysteriously disappear every time. So every couple of weeks, two human guys come by to handle the yard work for the parentals in this truck—yep, I see them now stepping out of the big vehicle, making quite a racket with their noisy tools. I can't tell you how many times I've been woken from a wonderful slumber to this nonsense. Today, I'm okay; I was already up, so it's not a big deal.

I figure it will take my brother a couple of seconds before he starts yapping to alert anyone within earshot of their presence. I only reach "one" before the barking begins. Ah, he's quicker than normal today. Usually, I would notify everyone as well, but I'm not in the mood and today will just stay at my desk and keep watch. When I post a notification, my alerts are specific, quick and on target. The terrier surprise is a little more manic. He tends to repeat the same thing over and over again. Even when a potential intruder has left the scene, he will go on for several more minutes. I can hear that Brother-Man has gone downstairs and is continuing to alert anyone interested. Honestly, the action is right here in front of me.

The two human guys have a system. They concentrate on the front of the house first. They stop to pick up the many leaves fallen at this time of year, pulling and clipping any unwanted weeds before removing the muncher of grass from the vehicle to trim up the yard. Now they've finished, so it's time for them to head around to the back through our gate. Ah, it's much quieter now, listening from the bedroom. There's only an echo coming from the backyard. My sibling, however, is still on alert. I can hear his bark coming and going. He must be pacing. We get it already, what is he going on and on about anyway?

"Buddy," I hear Dad say from downstairs. "Please keep it down." This is followed by some creaking on the steps. I turn and see Dad reach the second floor. Walking past my location and down the hall, he must be looking for quieter ground. After about a half an hour, the two human guys return to the front, pack up their gear and return to their vehicle. Something seems amiss, though. I know this because it is my job to be the eye in the sky, if you will. These two seem to be in a hurry today. Normally, they do an additional inspection of the front yard or ring the front bell—which as stated earlier I love—to chat with Mom about any issues or questions she may have. Today is different. With a clunk, they're back in the vehicle, which starts up and heads off down the street. Well, that's a fine how do you do. Where's the customer service? A dying art, I guess.

Still at my perch, I continue to hear Home Skillet yammering on and on downstairs. Of the many names I have for my brother, I particularly enjoy that one. This seems odd, even for him, as the yard humans are gone. Well, I'll go see what his problem is. I could use a break anyway from all this activity. Time for some coffee, go-go juice…okay, water it will be. From the top of the stairs, I hear the pitter patter of Buddy's feet on the hardwood floor below scampering about the kitchen. What is all the commotion? I arrive in the kitchen and head over to where Buddy is currently losing it, the sliding glass door facing the backyard, to see what's going on. Stop the presses! My furry little rabbit friend is back, and he's brought one of his cousins. Both are situated on the bench just above the fire pit. Oh, how I do love making new acquaintances. Drat! I can't get the door open to go out and say hello. Ding, ding, ding! I will get Mom. Keep an eye on them, Buddy, I'll be right back.

Since Mom works from home, I run back upstairs and head to her office, which is adjacent to mine. As I enter the room, I can see she's on the phone and looking at her computer monitor at the same time. Her monitor is considerably smaller than mine. Similar to the pane of knowledge but much smaller. She can only see odd symbols she calls words on hers, but she doesn't seem to mind, and makes up for this by having more than one. I've learned in the past it's best not to bother her while on a call. In my younger years, I would have burst in to her office eager to get her attention by any means necessary. This never ended well, with Mom escorting me out of the room and closing the door behind me. That was then. I'm more mature now. Hmm. This is super important, so I'm sure she won't mind. I need to bring my A game. "Mom, Mom, can I please, please go outside. Please, pretty please! Mom, Mom." I apply my paw to her leg. Subtle with just a hint of desperation.

Uh-oh, she seems a little annoyed, and quickly raises her hand for me to stop in my tracks. Drat, may have come on too strong. She tells whoever she is talking with to hold on. "What is it, Sydney?" she asks. "Do you need to take a break?" Why, yes, that'll work if it gets me outside. I hear my boy in the 'hood yammering on downstairs, so my furry friends must still be in sight.

"Yes, a break would be swell," I bark.

"Okay," she says. Still holding the phone, she walks toward the door. This is all the indication I need. I spring past her, zip down the stairs, and head over to the back door in no time.

A few seconds later, which seem like minutes, she finally catches up from behind. "You must really have to go. Buddy, you too? Okay, guys." She lifts the lock on the door, slides it open and out we go. Mom is the best.

CHAPTER 11

BUDDY

WHOA, HOLD THE PHONE! Fluffy tails, I see fluffy tails. I'm in the kitchen chugging down water as it splashes all over my face. Looking through the sliding glass door facing the backyard, I see two rabbits running around through my territory.

"Dudes, what are you doing here in my yard?" I bark. "Dudes, who gave you permission to be here? Dudes!" Hey, why aren't they paying attention to me? "Dudes!"

If at third you don't succeed, or is it second? Never been good with those phrases. First, if at first. Nailed it. Hey. Oh. The door is closed. Hmm, maybe they can't hear my commanding warning calls. I bark louder. "Dudes! Dudes! Dudes! What are you doing in my yard?" Pesky little guys, choosing to not look my way.

Decisions. It's time for some decisions. I stumble across the slick wood floor trying to remain upright, I'm so excited. Finally picking up speed, I bolt for the sofa and jump up on the cushions. Splat, I made it. From here, I can see the entire yard through the large clear windows. "I see you, I can see you there! I can still see you!" Hey, I also see a handsome looking terrier with blonde hair sporting a buzz type haircut. He's kind of invisible, though. Is he a ghost? Wait, that's just me. I look good. But back to the rabbits; I think these are the same fluffy tails I saw earlier today when I chased them off.

Squeak! What was that? I carefully adjust my position on the couch—okay, so not really, since I am a terrier, after all. Squeak! My back paw has stepped on a squeaky toy on the couch cushion. "Whoa, like what do we have here?" So bright in color. I must bite the yellow and green dinosaur. "I've got you, little dude," I say. Time stands still while I begin gnawing on my treasure. This time stuff is pretty advanced for a hound such as myself. Maybe that's why it's standing still. Whoa! Hmm, now my brain hurts. Squeak! This is awesome. My own toy to play with. Uh oh, I'm losing it. Suction, need more suction. Must try to clamp it down.

The dinosaur suddenly pops out of my mouth and shoots straight up in the air. I follow its progress and jump over a pillow in a single bound. It lands, bouncing off the end of my nose and against the nearby window. Window? Fluffy tails, I see fluffy tails. I've really got to work on this focusing thing.

Darting back to the door, I resume shouting at the rabbits. Hmm, it's still not working. If only I could get this door thingy open. "Who are you talking to, Buddy?" Uh oh, voices. I think I hear voices in my head.

"No, I'm over here," Sydney barks. Turning my head, I see my sister come about halfway down the stairs to see what all the commotion is about.

I tell her, "Tails! I've spotted the fluffy dudes from earlier today and can't stop moving. I'm so stoked!"

"Let me see!" Sydney enters the kitchen. She runs to the door. "Yes, there will be a sequel."

A what? "Got to run," she says as the runs past me toward the stairs.

I say, "Told you! Fluffy tails! Hey, where are you going?"

I don't know where she went but all this excitement makes me have to pee.

I hear Mom's voice say from upstairs. "Okay, Sydney, let's go." My sister has run upstairs to meet Mom. That sis of mine, she's so choice. Now, as they reach the bottom of the stairs, Mom opens the door and out we go. I do love the outdoors. The air is cool on my coat as I run across the paved patio and around to the right towards the grass. I love grass. On days when it's warmer, I like to flop down in the grass and run as fast as I can through the bushes. On sunny days, I find a nice spot and soak up the rays. Pops always tells me to stop, since I tend to come back inside smelling like the yard, but I can't help myself. I love grass. However, with the cooler air, the grass feels like bristles scraping my skin. Nah, brah, I don't like that.

From time to time, water will fall on me when I'm out back. I don't really like this much either. Pops calls it rain. On days like that, I do what I need to and run back to the house as soon as possible. But I don't smell it coming on today. Did I mention I can smell things really good? Nice! When Pops takes me for a walk I always keep my nose to the ground and can sniff out other hounds that live in our 'hood. There's the little white Scottish bloke, Dario, who lives two houses down. The English bull of a fellow, D-Dub, lives diagonal from my folks. 'Diagonal'—look at me rocking the big word. And that fierce tracker, TK, who lives down on the corner of our street. Wait, why am I out here again? Oh yeah, need to pee.

As I am a good and obedient boy, I do what I need to and head back to the slider and wait for Mom. Not sure what my sis is up to, but I'm content to chill here.

CHAPTER 12

SYDNEY

I FEEL LIKE I'M FLYING through the air at full speed on my Frisbee as we zoom out the sliding door. Before I know it, I clear the fire pit, jump on top of the concrete wall and ascend up the back hill toward my cotton-tailed potential friends. I should really look first before I start running with reckless abandon. I look around and quickly discover two things. One, Buddy hasn't followed me up the hill. Yes! My guesstimate was correct. He had to actually use the restroom. Two, I don't see my rabbit friends. Did they get scared off? Let's be clear, my intention is not to harm. Oh no, I'm a very social being and enjoy meeting new folks and learning about their lives. Since B-town hasn't figured what I'm doing, I will play it cool and just stroll around. I don't want a repeat performance of this morning. I need to be careful my brother doesn't interfere this time. Fool me once, shame on you. Fool me twice, I think not.

Mom is out of sight, so she must still be on the phone. Wandering around the top of the hill, I notice that Bud has gone back to the door and is staying put, waiting for her return. I casually saunter to the back corner of our yard, atop the hill, and I find myself at the same spot where my furry potential friends hopped out earlier this morning. By moving over here, I'm now out of Buddy's line of sight.

At this highest point in the yard, I look back and see the house. It does look beautiful from up here. Just a hint of sun bouncing off the back windows, and the leaves from the morning are all gone thanks to the cleanup by the yard humans. All that remains of their visit are footprints in the slightly damp grass. I look along the stone path on the side of the house—a new addition Mom and Dad added last spring—and discover one of my would-be new friends. Blocked by the green garbage bin, from this angle and distance I can see him, but so far he hasn't detected my presence. He sure looks tiny from this vantage point. The stone path is offset with fragrant flowers, and one in particular has attracted the attention of my soon-to-be friend. The furry little guy has an almost maroon coat and black stripes zigzagging all over its body, and is admiring one of Mom's plants. Patience, oh wise one. Deep breaths. Keep still.

Hey, I see another new potential lifelong pal emerge from behind the garden hose rolled up on the ground to join this cotton-tailed ball of energy. The new guy can't seem to sit still and is practically hopping in place. Even I'm starting to lose my cool now. Two of them—this is awesome. This is it, I'm going for it. New friends, here I come.

I zoom down the hill and head towards the stone pathway. Yes! I make it safely to the ground level and...oh no...the furry ones spot me and run in the opposite direction, towards the front of the house. Hah, I've got them, as there aren't a lot of options with the gate closed. I make my way over to the path, but I've temporarily lost them. What, how? Of course, the gate is open. It should be closed, but without taking time to wonder why it's not, or think about the consequences of getting caught by the parentals, I run through the entry toward the front of the yard. Ah, this is what freedom feels like. My ninja-like cockapoo reflexes make it easy to navigate the front portion of the yard. I quickly survey the area and catch a glimpse of the rabbits again as they head straight from our house, sprint about 50 feet across the drive, and up a hill toward some bushes. No time like the present; it's time to give chase, I tell myself. I run across the drive in front of my house, and I'm up the adjoining hill in no time. I almost catch up to them as I make it to the entry of the bushes that separate the neighborhood from the woods. Ah, the great outdoors.

I hear branches crackle up ahead, seeming to indicate the position of my hard-to-get-hold of new friends. Man! This making-new-friends thing is a lot more difficult than I ever imagined it would be. I continue further into the woods looking for those fluffy guys. I spy them just ahead, and stepping over a few tree trunks, I catch up to the first bouncy guy. I've never talked to another type of animal other than my brother and other dogs. Well, here goes nothing. "Hello," I tell him with my bark. "I'm Sydney. I don't mean to scare or hurt you. I just like meeting new folks and saw you in my yard and want to be your friend. Will you be my new friend? What's your name?"

"What are you doing out here?" asks my new friend. "You're not supposed to be out here. You could get me into a lot of trouble."

Ah, he can understand me, but he seems to be new to friend making. "I just wanted to say hello and hang out," I say. "Did I catch you at a bad time?"

"Catching up to me is part of the problem, yes. We don't like your kind out here."

"I'm sorry, my what? Most folks love my kind, thank you very much." Perhaps my translation is a little rusty. Otherwise, this is not the best foot to get off on while attempting a new friendship.

"Do you know what an inner circle is?"

"Yes, silly question." It looks like he just rolled his eyes at me. Hmm, may have insulted the little guy. "Er, inner circle you say? Go on."

"How would you define yours?"

"My parentals and my brother, I suppose."

"You keep close together, do you?" the furry little one asks.

"Oh, yes, we are family."

"Well, same here. And out here, the circle is especially tight. If we're not careful, we could lose a member of that unit. Understand?"

"I guess, but what does that have to do with me? I just want to be your friend."

"Well, I'm not allowed to make new friends. That type of bonding hasn't turned out well in the past. It's best to not let anyone in, for fear of losing them down the line. Unless you're family, we make no lasting relationships."

I watch as the other furry little pal begins to head toward our location from deeper in the woods. Still hopping, he says, "Hey! Hey, Ed!"

The first rabbit turns his way. "Shush, I said no names. The code, stick to the code. What is it?"

"They're coming."

"What. Now?"

"Yep, we need to skedaddle."

Ed turns back to me. "Look, it's been nice meeting you, Sydney," he says. "We've got some—how should I put it?—issues out here, and I don't have time to get into it. I've got to hop. You would be wise to go back to your dwelling."

"What? But I haven't met your pal yet, and I still don't know what all of this is about."

Before I am able to finish my response, the bushes crack behind us and two big deer emerge on the woodsy path. Normally, the deer seem pleasant from a distance, but my spidey senses are tingling. Breathing heavily, the first deer stops in its tracks. The rather large brown doe proceeds to dig its hoof into the ground a couple of times while slowly lowering its head into what I'm guessing is not a "what's up" pose. Quickly, I figure out why. A big grayish brown coyote is approaching from the other side. The menacing figure growls at Ed, Al, the deer and me.

"The dog is mine," says the coyote. Well, apparently I can understand coyotes as well. Sure, the one time my cunning intellect comes back to get me. I start to shiver and wish I had gone to the bathroom earlier. Not my best Kodak moment. The nose of the second deer seems inflamed and he is breathing heavier than his compadre. Both of them study us at first, and then the coyote, for what seems like a very long second. Hmm, so this is what a stand-off is like. I feel like the rabbits and I have come between something we shouldn't have. The first deer motions with its head at us as if to say, "Make a run for it," and then starts to lunge at the coyote.

"Well, Sydney, you're with us now," Ed says. "We've got to make a break for it. Follow me."

"Yay!" New adventure and two new friends all in one day. Sweet. I'll have to work on the deer friendship later. Still on the fence about the coyote.

CHAPTER 13

BUDDY

MOM PREPARES TO LET me back inside after my break. "Buddy, come on in." A quick slide of the back door and I am ready. Excellent! Being the good boy that I am, I dart right inside and can't help but spin in circles around Mom, I'm so excited to see her. It's been…well, it seems like a long time since I saw her last.

Mom says, "Okay, Bud, calm down, where's your sister?"

That is a very good question. Mom is so smart. "I don't know," I bark. Last I saw her, she was in the backyard, just like me.

Mom goes outside to call for her again and I go with, to help. "Sydney, Sydney!" I'm good at helping, plus I follow Mom just about everywhere she goes. "Where could she be?" Mom wanders out a bit further into the backyard and continues her search. Sis always comes when Mom calls, so this seems a bit odd. I want to be of assistance, so I use my keen sense of smell and keep my nose to the back patio. I smell the scent of the fluffy tails that were in the yard earlier. Oh, boy, fluffy tails! I follow the scent trail over to the side of the house, near the stone pathway. I also pick up the scent of my sister in this same area and see a couple of her paw prints.

"Over here," I bark to Mom. She's still on the other side of the yard looking for Sydney. I follow the smell as it continues back toward the fence. That's weird. The gate door that is usually closed is open. Mom is not going to be happy about that. She and Pops like to keep the door closed so my sis and I don't wander out or other critters come in. Wait a minute. Whoa! Dude! No way! I think she ran out through the open gate door. I can hear Sydney's voice in my head now, saying, "Do you think so?" Did I just figure something out? Sweet! "Mom! Momma! Mommy!" I run over to her, trying to let her know what I've found. "C'mere! Found something! Found something!"

"What is it, Buddy?" Mom walks with me as I lead her to the other side of the house. She sees the open gate door and cries, "Oh no! Sydney!"

Mom's tone changes, and she seems very concerned. She runs through the door and out toward the front of the house. I go right along with her.

Wow, the front yard. I've only been out here a few times but never off leash, like now. Usually, when Mom and Pops are getting ready to travel somewhere in the big red wagon, we are led to and from on the leash, and I make a point to bark at any passerby who is out and about. I'm still working on my social skills. "Social." Look at me again with words and stuff. Bonus, Mom is here, so extra credit for me.

"I don't see her anywhere," Mom says. Her tone is a bit more frantic now. I see tears in her eyes.

I try to make her feel better. "Don't worry, Mom. I still have her scent and I'm on the trail. Nothing to fear when the Bud-man is here."

CHAPTER 14

SYDNEY

FOLLOWING ED AND HIS FRIEND deeper into the woods proves to be a little tricky. These two have clearly done this before. Ed's furry pal is pressing forward, keeping a rock-solid steady beat to the groove in the trail which we're all laying down. Ed, on the other hand, is bouncing back and forth. Sometimes he darts out in front and takes the lead; other times, he is in lock step next to me. I've never seen a critter move so quickly and with such ease, bounding and tapping across the landscape. His friend has the same easy way of moving. Okay, so technically I haven't been introduced to the other little guy, but my ability to keep up with them should go a long way in establishing my level of awesomeness. After all,

I'm right on their fluffy tails and when I glance back for a quick second, the deer and combative looking coyote are nowhere to be found.

Ed and his friend jump off the trail and head into some thicker brush that leads us down a steep grade. They pause. "We should be safe here," Ed says taking a minute to catch his breath.

"Wow, how cool was that?" I ask, taking a moment myself to let my heart rate calm down a bit. "I don't think I've been out this far from the house before." I won't lie, it's a little scary and equally fun.

"Not that cool at all," Ed's pal chimes in.

"So you *do* speak," I say. "I'm sorry, we've not been formally introduced. I'm Sydney. Would you be my new friend? I love making new friends."

Ed interjects, "You can call him Al, and don't get too excited. He's my brother."

"Got it. Brother. I know what those are like." I nod at Ed.

"Look, you just messed up our entire routine," Ed continues. "We work really hard to keep a low profile out here. We stick to our own territory and don't play with outsiders. Your little introduction into our world has upset the balance we work toward, as evidenced by that standoff. We haven't had an issue like this since the construction obstruction. The coyote has been away all season and the day you show up in our world we get a visit from it. Now we need to undo what you started. I'm going to have to explain this to the deer."

"What? We're just getting to know each other." I say to them both. "Besides, how are you going to undo this anyway?"

"You need to go home, that's how."

"Wait, fellas, we're just getting to know each other. It's rare that I get outside my yard, and when I'm at home, you never seem to want to chat when you hop in and out. What's the deal?"

Al begins to chirp, "Well, that's because…"

Ed interrupts. "I've got this, Al. You go and keep a look out for any intruders." Al hops off and Ed turns back to me. "Sydney, my brother and I stick together. We don't mingle with you, or anyone else for that matter, since we lost Big Papa. Our little family used to all hang out with the deer when there was a wide open space instead of another house next to your home. Deer are quite peaceful, and a little absent minded. We often enjoyed searching for food together and running freely through the grass. As the lot became full of tools, lumber and equipment from the construction, it became harder and harder to find food. Big Papa, our dad, decided to expand the search. We all hopped in and around the noisy gizmos and scraps of wood making our way to a hillside just beyond the group of houses. As this was uncharted territory, Big Papa told us to stay put as he went to check and survey the area for any potential threats. He was hopping over some rocks along the perimeter to make his way up the adjacent hillside. Halfway up, he landed on a collection of twigs and branches. His weight on the pile caused him to start to sink right in front of our eyes. He tried to hop but the hillside was collapsing around him, which exposed a den that a bear was using to hibernate for the winter. Papa never returned home."

"A bear den?" I said.

"When my brother and I were little we thought, like everyone else, that bears just built and hibernated in caves. Papa was just covering the area, and none of us realized dens could also be built on a hillside. When they're there, the ground gets unstable, so you always need to be on your toes. We learned that the hard way."

"I had no idea," I said.

"Look Sydney, I like you. You seem cool. But you also invite an element of trouble we just don't need. I've been down that path before, and it doesn't end well. And, well, my brother is all I have left now, and I can't chance losing him. You mentioned you have a family, right? I'm sure you can understand not wanting to lose your parents or brother, correct?"

I have never given that much thought. "I do love my parents, but my brother can be annoying. He's always playing with my stuff, and he hogs all the attention of my parentals."

"Poor pitiful Pearle. It sounds like a tough life there for you in your own home with actual ceilings and I can only guess, central heat."

"Oh, yes, I do love the heat and warmth when I sit and cozy up against the fireplace. In the summer, we even have cool air running through the house. Dad calls it the A-Slash-C. Wait a minute. Did I miss something? Who is Pearle, again?"

"Look, kid," Ed continues bouncing back and forth. "You've got what sounds like an amazing pad, and folks who care about you. Al and I aren't as lucky out here in these mean backwoods streets. We fend for ourselves, and have to burrow our own little domicile in the ground for shelter and to keep warm.

"Don't get me wrong, I like life here. It's all I've ever known. But I'm guessing it's not what you've experienced. We saw you and your brother earlier when we were in your yard shopping for dinner. Your mom and dad provide food and water for you. Out here, you have to do that for yourself, and sometimes you miss meals because there's nothing to be found. I've found it difficult to trust new folks, so it's best to just stay separate and mind our own business."

Ed gets real quiet and lowers his head to the side a little. I walk up a little closer to him. I've never been this close to the furry guy before. Parts of his hair are torn, maybe caught on something or by someone; his nails are uneven; and, whoa, he could probably use a bath. At home, watching them through the monitor window, I envisioned how fun it must be to run around freely, and do what you want when you want, rather than having to beg to go o-u-t. But getting a taste of outdoor life today, I think I prefer to be home in my house with Mom, Dad, and extended family and friends like River and the girls. Heck, I would even include my brother Buddy in the mix. Shh, we will never speak of that last sentence again.

I lean over and give Ed a quick lick on his head. "Ed, you and your brother are welcome in my yard anytime. Next time I see you both, I will ask the parentals for some treats. I will then sneak, sneak, sneak a couple for you and Al."

"Hey, I don't want to attract too much attention and put you out," Ed comments. "And I don't want to get you or your brother into any unwanted trouble. I appreciate the offer, but you don't have to do all of that for us."

I nose his cheek. "Um, in case you didn't notice, the three of us are now besties. And I don't know about you, but in my world, you look after your friends and help them out if you can. I can, and I will."

"I appreciate that," Ed replies. "Al and I won't forget this. Sydney, I was wrong about you. I'm sorry we didn't say hello to you and make friends earlier. We've gotten burned in the past by other critter folk, and sadly, we labeled you before actually getting to know you. But I can safely say, you are the coolest cat we've come across."

"Thanks," I say. "And FYI, I'm a dog."

"Oh, right, my bad." He calls to Al, a few feet away. "Al, how does it look?"

"All clear. The deer seem to have fended off the coyote and are long gone," Al says.

"Al, Sydney here is one of the good ones. I was wrong about her and I can now say with assurance, she is part of our social group and a trusted friend."

"Nice to have you on board, Sydney," says Al, hopping up to me with his paw extended. I quickly high five him back.

"You guys are cool," I say. "Hey, I probably should get back before my parentals notice I'm missing. They've tended to not like it when I've gotten out in the past."

"Okay," said Al, "we'll help you find your way back home. We're quite a ways from your pad."

Before we have a chance to head out, the ground under our feet starts to soften, feeling loose under my paws. Some of the leaves and branches begin to slide and the ground starts to slip away. An opening forms, presenting a big black hole to nowhere.

"Bear den!" Ed shouts.

I watch as Ed and Al hop up and out in time, but I wait just a second too long and slip away from where we were into what is now becoming a larger and larger void. Calm down, Syd, get it together. Breathe. Do. Not. Panic. If I can just... there, that's a little better. I steady myself and manage to secure my footing. Ok—it's going to be ok. My relief is short lived. The ground beneath my paws gives way and I fall into darkness.

CHAPTER 15
SYDNEY

BLACKNESS. As far as the eye can see, it is only dark and black. It's like my eyes aren't even open. Wait—are my eyes open? Nope. I open my eyes to get my bearings. Okay, that's better. I feel like I'm wearing one of those Christmas sweaters Mom gets for my brother and me, only this sweater would be three times too small. I'm packed in here pretty good. What's that? I feel what I'm guessing are leaves covering my body, based on the texture brushing against my nose and mouth. My back paws seem positioned between a rock and what feels like branches digging into my side. I'm also getting a very strong scent of—could that be?—Twinkies. Huh, they do last forever. I am a D-O-double G, you know; I'm good at stuff like this. Look at me using a 90's rap reference from the Dogfather, Snoop Dogg. Dad's not here so I can get away with that reference.

Looking straight ahead, I think, darkness is all I see, as I'm covered by dirt and debris. The air doesn't feel particularly cool, but cozy isn't the right word either. Trapped, that's the word. I'm trapped in this den with just my thoughts. "Trapped" is such an ugly word, perhaps "stuck." Yes, "stuck" sounds much more positive. "Positive," another good word. Try to stay positive. Well, girl, you've really gone and done it to yourself this time. Wait. That's not a helpful attitude. I muster up all of my will and work to pull myself together. By doing so, I understand I can't take this situation lying down, or however I'm positioned. I shake my head back and forth enough to push the riffraff back, and expose my face to a small ray of sunlight. I still can't seem to move the rest of my body. But I don't feel hurt, which is great news.

From my vantage point, I can't tell where I am, and Ed and Al are long gone due to the shuffle. Is this how they define friendship? We need to talk the next time I see them, if… Okay, positive is the word of the day. Maybe they were scared off and are coming back for me? Maybe they went to get help? Maybe this is a dream and I'm at home asleep on my bed? Honestly, I wouldn't blame them if they did take off—this is pretty hairy stuff. Pun, not intended this time. Although? I try to bark, hoping someone will hear and come find me. I mean, who doesn't love a damsel in distress? But it seems that isn't possible either. The pressure against my body limits me to just inhaling and exhaling. I'm a little worried.

I never realized how quiet it is out here in the woods. Now I know the answer to that age old question. If a cockapoo falls in the woods, does she make a sound? Apparently not. The great outdoors seemed so exciting from inside the house looking out. The mystery of what is just over that hill. The action of where those cars go when they drive down the street. The element of danger. Okay, I didn't plan on actual danger.

I can hear Dad now in my head: "You shouldn't wander off, Sydney. You could get into trouble." He's always telling Buddy and me that it's better to be safe. I always figured that was just a speech he prepared; I never thought it would ever actually apply to me. I can't believe I'm going to say this, but listen to your parentals. It could save you from situations and explanations you're not ready to give, like this one.

Now that it appears that Ed and Al have run off, I feel so helpless and alone. Wait, Ed mentioned this was a bear den. Is the bear coming back? Does he know I'm here? I'm a sitting duck, well, cockapoo. However, since the den seems to have crumbled around me, I don't think a bear could find me any longer. I listen closely to see if I can hear anyone else in the area to assist me. Crickets. Well, not actual crickets, but you get the idea. Literally nothing. Not even a cricket. What am I going to do now? I'm all alone, there's no one in sight, and no way to communicate. A sense of loneliness sinks in. Keep it together, Syd, I tell myself. I've never been away from the house unsupervised this long before. You know, being pinned under a tree branch out in the woods somewhere near your house, or maybe not, gives you some time to think about your life.

I miss my Mom. When I'm sick or feeling blue, like now, she always spends time with me and lets me cuddle with her. She somehow knows when I'm down and provides support for me with what she calls "a puppy cuddle." And when I need medicine, she always puts it in peanut butter. Normally, I would say yum when talking about or recalling my favorite snack, but I can only think it now, what with this awful pressure on my chest. Mom has been with me for as long as I can remember, since I was a puppy. She always plays with me, and is always there to throw a squeaky ball or crawl around with me on the floor when it gets stuck under the couch. We sing together. "Sydney," she will say. "Can you sing?" she will ask as she raises her voice on the word "sing." I attempt to sing with her but always feel I'm more howling than singing. She even has a photograph of me framed on the wall for all to see when I went through that cheerleader phase. If she were here, I know she wouldn't be upset with me. She would be happy to see me, and I her, and she would wrap a big hug around me. I could use that hug right now. A single tear slips from my eye. I miss my mom.

I miss my dad too. The two of them met a couple of years after I was around. To be honest, when I heard he was coming over for the first time, I was worried. I thought I would get relegated to the background, and only see her at meals, collecting treats from time to time, while her attention switched to Dad. But when I met my future dad on that initial visit, he brought pink roses for my mom, and he brought a squeaky toy for yours truly as a gift, too. I knew he was a keeper from that very minute. My relationship with my dad is awesome. We hang out all the time. He gives me snacks when Mom isn't looking. He lets me pick channels to watch on the pane of knowledge like those music shows Mom won't watch. *And* he throws the ball for me anytime I ask. Sometimes, I don't even have to ask—he's that cool. When he asked my mom to marry him, he didn't just stop there. Oh no, he had a present for me as well. It was a beautiful plush blue and pink box. Dad opened it up for me to see and inside was a soft squeaky toy ring to match Mom's. He's a keeper, right? Right! I miss him as well. Another tear slips from my eye.

Just prior to their wedding came the little monster that is my brother Buddy. Have I expressed various issues with him? Good. Just checking. I won't bother you with any sordid details because I'm actually feeling a bit tired at the moment. This dirt and junk sure weigh a lot. Truth be told, I miss him as well. He may be a thorn in my side, but he's *my* thorn. Silly terrier, he seems to do things his own wacky way. Known for inhaling his food, this can require a sudden trip outside afterward if not careful. The food, well let's just say it doesn't always stay in his stomach. Mom and Dad are always concerned for him and usher him out back really quick to not make a mess on the floor. They will stand at the window to watch and make sure he is okay. I know this because I've stood there too. I even pawed my mom for a quick cuddle. I get scared for him. Turns out, he's always fine and the little bugger is back inside in a couple of minutes. I miss my family. They are the most important thing in the world to me. I love them more than anything.

Wait…Buddy. He came outside with me when Mom let us out. Did he see where I went? Does he know I'm missing? Does he remember my name? To be fair, these are all viable questions. Like the girl with the cinnamon rolls on her ears says: "Help me, little Buddy, you're my only hope."

CHAPTER 16
BUDDY

SNIFFING AROUND, I'm picking up a stronger scent for the fluffy tails and faint traces of Sydney. It smells like they ran across the front of the house and up the hill just ahead of us. I turn to tell Mom what I've found. Just then, I see the fluffy tails across from the house on top of the hill. "Fluffy tails, I see fluffy tails!" I spring across the front of the house and head toward the hill. The fluffy tails turn and disappear into the brush.

"I see you, and better yet, I can smell you and my sis." I'm on the hunt now. As I reach the top of the hill, I can hear Mom from below telling me to stop. I don't like to disobey her, but I'm onto something here. Turning quickly, I bark, "I've got this," and with a quick head bob, I'm off.

Just inside the brush, I lose sight of the fluffy tails. No problem, I will sniff them out. Picking up the scent, I move swiftly through the woods and feel the crackling of tree branches under my paws.

Starting to get lots of different smells now. I smell chocolate, crackers and, I think, Twinkies. In my former life, I encountered antenna heads that Mom calls "deer" and big burly guys I know now are "bears." Cause for concern as I am detecting antennas and something—not exactly bear, but I don't know what—and they look to have followed the fluffy tails and my sis for a while. Smells like I missed a good time. Bummer! I continue into the woods on the search for my sister. She's out here and I will find her. Stopping in my tracks where the trail breaks off, I hear the crackling of footsteps coming from my right. Yep, I smell antennas, and they're headed my way. No sooner do I figure this out than two antenna heads cross my path from the woods and move directly in front of me.

"Dudes," I say to break the ice cube tray. Wait, that's not it. Oh, break the ice. "Dudes, I come in peace and I mean you no harm."

"Mean us no harm," repeats AH1, as I quickly name him in my head. "Do you realize there are two of us and we are considerably larger than you?"

"Dudes, I am a terrier and back down from no one, or two of you, in this case. My name is

Buddy and I'm out here looking for my sister. I have no beef with you. Have you seen a white fluffy cockapoo answering to the name Sydney?"

"Maybe. What's it to you, little man?"

Jokers, I see. Well, it's time to get serious with these two, as I am in a hurry and every minute wasted leads to a cold trail.

Walking toward AH1, I see two tree trunks at varying heights just to his left. I consider jumping up for a more forceful stance. Why, though? I'm a tough little guy and this is my wooded area as much as it is theirs. I decide to hold my own. "Dudes, as I mentioned, I'm a terrier on the lookout for my missing sister, and don't have time to get into it with both of you. Have you seen her?" I ask again.

"Come on, dawg, we're just playing with you. We saw her and a couple of rabbits an hour ago during the coyote encounter."

 Coyote. That's what I smelled. "Is everyone okay?"

"More of our friends were on the way and the coyote ran off into the woods. We attempted to give chase to the rabbits and your sister, but they lost us a little ways back. However, we've learned not to mess with terriers, and we respect the fact you're searching for a lost family member. How can we help?"

"First of all," I say, "I only play with my sister, or Mom and Pops when squeaky toys are involved. I see no toys out here. Second, when you say rabbits, do you mean fluffy tails?" Wait. I forgot what's after second. Focus. Got it. "Third, I'm good at tracking but could use your help, since I don't know these woods." The trail seems to have gone cold here and I don't want to have to circle back.

Deciding to pool our resources (where's Pops now, he would be so proud of my vocabulary), we double back, looking for my sis.

CHAPTER 17

SYDNEY

EXPLORING THE WOODS always seemed like a fun idea, but being stuck in this black hole, helpless and alone, really changes the meaning for me. This could be some sort of medieval torture device if it wasn't actually present day. My entire body itches after being poked by twigs. My mind is consumed with thoughts of home when I have an itch I just can't scratch, and how great it is to just roll around on the carpet, trying to slide along as if I'm swimming, feeling the warm soft fibers on my body, until I find that sweet relief. Oh, and I'm sure I'm filthy now. I can't imagine laying in this hole is good for my coat. I am definitely going to need a bath after all of this is done. Maybe I will head to the spa with Mom for one of those pedicures. I mean pet-i-cure. Even though I'm stuck in the middle of nowhere with no form of rescue, I've got my humor to keep me company. Yep, still got it.

My mom and I have had some pretty great times. She has even accepted my not-so-great moments. Keep in mind, these moments were when I was little. Although, this grit coating in my fur reminds me of one of my not-so-great moments, and takes me back to the days of flour power. I remember the floor still gritty on my feet and covered in white dust detailing my path as I heard the front door lock starting to turn. Mom would be inside in just a matter of moments. Try to look cute, I thought, this is going to sting a bit.

Several years back, I was just a puppy. Still learning my way around, I wasn't quite familiar with the lay of the land and needed some extra supervision. Well, that's what Mom said, anyway. I remember how in those first few months with Mom, she would head off to work during the day and leave me sequestered in the kitchen. Or locked up. It all depends on how you look at it. A baby gate blocked one entrance to the kitchen and my crate sat at the other end. Well, did you ever spend a day in the kitchen with nothing to do? Sucks, doesn't it? Still, nobody ever said I wasn't creative. You'd be surprised what you can do with several hours on your paws and a pantry nearby and an excellent nose. One day, I saw a bag with the letters F-L-O-U and R. It smelled really good and it happened to be within reach. Mom would never know if I snuck a little, or so I thought. As I've come to learn, Mom always knows. How does she do that?

Left to my own devices, and sensing the time was right, I reached out with my right front paw for the bag on the second to lowest shelf of the pantry. The almost blinding white and blue package looked so appealing. Ooh! Drat, I couldn't seem to pull it from the shelf. It was just a tad too high for my small frame. Still, while making my unsuccessful first attempt, I noticed that the shelf moved a bit, causing the package to sway back and forth. Rule number one: a cockapoo never gives up. I purposefully bumped the shelf harder a second time. The bag started to sway back and forth. Ha, now we're talking. Using my paw as a guide, down the bag came to the floor with a thud.

It was in that second that I realized knocking the bag over might not have been a good idea. Seeing things from beginning to end was not my strong suit when I was young. Ok, maybe it's still not, even though I'm older. Learning something new every day.

I watched the bag fall from the shelf but I didn't factor in how I would catch it. I also didn't realize the bag was open. Suddenly, white dust began to fall, like snow from above inside the kitchen; it coated my fur, the floor and just about everything else in its wake. Only, this wasn't snow. The explosion seemed to stop time. It was nothing but a white cloud passing overhead. I was unable to react. For a minute, I was blinded as if I were stuck in a whiteout on one of those shows about Alaska.

After the storm passed, I stood looking at the devastation. It was eerily quiet now; not even the sound from the fridge could be heard in the room. This quiet was followed by an itching in my nose that caused me to sneeze. Not just once, but over and over again. The white stuff was now in my nasal passages. During the collision, the bag had torn open even more and this white powdery substance had spilled all over the floor. What now? I realized I'd better clean this up before Mom comes home. No worries, I thought, I will just use my tongue as a mop. Win-win. Clean floor and I will have a nice treat to boot. As I began licking, though, I made an unpleasant discovery, what is this stuff? It smells so much better than it tastes. Still, I figured the snack would get tastier; I continued to eat it and in my attempt to do so, I spilled a smidge more on the floor. This, of course, depends on your definition of smidge.

Trouble. Why did my throat feel like it was drying up so quickly? It was like I couldn't swallow. No, it was *exactly* like that. I really couldn't swallow. Water, where was the water? Panic started to set in.

I managed to find my way to the water through the white-capped miniature mountains. Gulp, gulp. The water started to help. I needed more. Gulp, gulp. Okay, I was starting to feel a little better. That was a close one. Gulp, gulp. Yay! I could swallow again. Maintaining my breathing, I had a little more water and started to calm down. Whoops, did I just drink all the water? Well, at least I was feeling better, and really, that was the important part here. Surely Mom would understand I was a little thirsty, hence why all my water was gone. Surely. Unfortunately, that didn't explain everything.

B-bump, b-bump. My heart was pounding in my chest now. Throat: dry. Water bowl: empty. What felt like a thick coating of water combined with the white stuff had dried onto my beard, leaving it feeling clumpy and hard. The bag of F-L-O-U and R was torn in pieces and strewn about the kitchen floor. White, powder-kissed tiles decorated the kitchen floor. Paw prints left a trail as if I had been walking in the snow. Follow the evidence. "No worries, this is all manageable," I said to myself as if to somehow reassure. Wait, I'd already proved it wasn't. I couldn't eat any more, as the dryness in my mouth and empty bowl could attest to. I couldn't pick up the bag, as A) I didn't have thumbs and B) the trash was outside my play area.

And then, to make things worse, I heard a car pull up toward the front of the house. Definitely, I now heard the sound of the garage door opening and vehicle shutting off. Mom was home. Oh, no. What would I do now? She was not going to be excited about my little escapade. I was done for. I could hear her fiddling with the keys to open the door. Quickly, I tried to brush the white stuff away with my paws. Nope, now my paws were white. I had only been with my Mom for a short while, and look at the destruction I'd left in my wake in just one afternoon. All I could think of as I heard that lock on the door open was: just smile and try to look cute. My lips were stuck together. Just be cute.

Mom came in the house and at first didn't see the carnage. She stopped at the closet to put her coat away, prolonging the inevitable. Turning toward the kitchen, she said, "Where's my Syd…" Yeah, that last part dropped off. I saw disappointment on her face for the first time. It was not a good feeling. "Someone got into the flour today, didn't they," she said in an authoritative tone. I didn't really have a response for that one. I was busted and I knew it.

Mom walked past me to the sink. She got some towels made of paper and started to wipe off my face. "Well, Sydney, those cookies I was going to make will have to wait until another day. Looks like you need a bath." She picked me up and carried me upstairs to the bathroom. After letting the water run for just a minute, she placed me in the tub. The water was nice and warm on my skin and Mom helped to get all the white stuff off of me. With the rinse done, she turned off the water and used a soft towel to wipe me off. To Mom's credit, she never flipped out or raised her voice. No, she was just glad I hadn't gotten sick, and after she cleaned up the mess downstairs, she gave me a big hug and a kiss. I can confirm I never got into the flour again.

Mom is the great forgiver, as she proved that day. I can laugh about that story now, as it provides some comfort out here on my own. If she were here, we would laugh together. She has a great laugh. I miss that right now. I've done some silly things before, and probably will again—just as soon as someone figures out where I am. Dad says it's good to always stay positive. I hope whoever it is finds me soon. I may need more than just a bath and tidy after this kerfuffle.

CHAPTER 18

BUDDY

NOSE, DON'T FAIL ME NOW. What is that? Getting a stronger scent now. "Hold up," I tell the antennas. "I hear something rustling. Keep quiet and don't say a word."

"Psst, over here!"

"Hey, antennas, what did I say? Keep it down, okay?" Sheesh.

"It wasn't us," says the second antenna head.

I'm confused. "If it wasn't you, am I hearing things again?"

A voice chirps, "No. Down here."

I look down. One of the fluffy tails pokes its head out from the brush. "Fluffy tail, I've found the fluffy tail!" I exclaim.

"Calm down, man," says the fluffy tail. "You're Sydney's brother, right?"

"Dude, how do you know who I am? Can you read minds? What number am I thinking of?"

"I met your cockapoo earlier today. I'm Ed."

"Yes, she is my sister and I'm out here with my bros, the antennas."

"Who?" asks Ed.

"Where are my manners?" I say. "AH1, Ed, AH2, Ed, Ed, AH1, Ed, AH2." Phew, that's quite a tongue twister.

"We know these two," says Ed. "We go way back and have history together."

"History," Buddy says. "That's like in the past, right?"

"Indeed," says Ed. "I'm glad you're here, Buddy. We can use your help. When the deer distracted the coyote, we managed to escape and got away. However, your sister got stuck in what I think was a bear den, and we need to get her out of there. We came looking for help. What do you say, guys?"

"We don't normally like confrontation," said AH1. "But given our day so far, why not. We don't want to see harm come to the little dog."

A second fluffy tail hops up and stands next to Ed. "I hate to break up the party," he says. "I circled back and think I've found her."

"Fluffy tail, I found another fluffy tail!"

"Buddy," says Ed. "This is my brother Al. Where did you see her?"

"Follow me," says Al.

Whoa, in a short amount of time, not a minute so I'm going with an hour, I've met two antennas who turned out to be super cool, and now two fluffy tails. This day is getting better and better. Wait, I still have to find my sis. "Okay, everyone, follow me."

"Buddy," said Ed. "Do you know where she is?"

"Excellent point," I replied. "Okay, everyone, follow Al."

We follow Al up to the edge of a steep grade. As we trot and hop along, Al explains that Sydney came here with the two of them when suddenly, the ground beneath them started to shift, and with the movement of the earth, her body got pulled under.

"We got lucky," says Al. "Because we're so light, we were able to hop away. Otherwise, we would have been pulled down too. This is the last place we saw her."

"I'm good at tracking," I say to the group. "Let me take a sniff." If Sydney has been here, I will do my best to find her. I hope she is okay. I walk up to where Al is and sniff around. Bing, I got it! She was here! I alert the guys and continue to search for her. Taking a quick look around, I see the side of a hill that has given way, branches and leaves everywhere. I jump over to a mound of dirt a few feet away, to sturdier ground. Al and Ed are just behind me. Whatever was here on this hill seems to have collapsed. Drat, I've lost the scent. But she must be close. "Guys, spread out and see if you can see her." Meanwhile, I circle back to find the antennas who remain on higher ground. These antennas are pretty good at keeping watch. "Dudes, I think she's down here. If you head back down over here around two tree trunks a bit, you won't have to worry about losing your footing on this hill."

"No problem, B-man," say the antennas.

"Got something. I think I see her," says Al hopping at the edge of tree line.

I jump back down the hill and run over to Al. "What is it? Did you find her?" Looking just beyond Ed, in and amongst the short and broken branches, I see a little black nose surrounded by white fur, but no movement. She's a fighter, I tell myself. She'll be okay. Several more branches are laying across her body. The antennas approach from the other side.

"Okay, guys, let's see if we can dig her out," I say. Ed and Al work to pick up all the loose leaves with their front paws and gently brush away the dirt so we can see her face. The antennas attempt to use their long legs to move some branches. Pressing their shoulders together to keep upright, they work as a team and begin to push bits away around her location while I start to dig her out. Slowly I am able to remove dirt from around her head. Ed and Al work to cut an outline in the dirt of her body, so that she can move a little. I gently grab the soft skin above her shoulder blades using my teeth and start to pull her loose. The antennas use their legs lifting her up.

Finally, we are able to free her. The branches and dirt fall away from her body, but her eyes remain closed. Together, we move her away from the remains and set her on solid ground. Why isn't she moving? Oh no, we're too late! How will I explain this to Mom? Just when I am about to give up all hope, she starts to cough and slowly opens her eyes. Whoa, that was close. She had me worried for a second. I bark, "Are you okay? Can you move?" After a second, Sydney shakes some of the rubble from her body. She begins to move and looks straight at me.

"What took you so long, Buddy?"

Yep, she is fine.

CHAPTER 19

SYDNEY

"DID I MISS SOMETHING?" I ask. "Are we having a party?" Silence falls over the group surrounding me in the woods. Tough crowd, I think. "I'm fine, really, I am. Who's going to help me up?" Buddy comes over to lend a paw.

"I was worried about you and stuff," says Buddy, helping me stand. He places his head under my stomach as I work to use my legs. "Mom discovered the gate was open and you were missing. I met these cool dudes here in the woods and together we were able to track you down. Pretty radical, if I do say so myself."

My thoughts shift to Mom and Dad for a quick second. I hope I'm not in too much trouble. "How long have I been gone?" I ask.

"Um, I'm not good with time, but it seems like several centons," Buddy comments. "Whoa, did you all hear that? Excellent!"

Buddy watches the original *Battlestar Galactica* on DVD, as I've come to learn on the pane of knowledge. Does he even know centons are minutes? He tries, I'll give him that. I chat with my new friends and discover that Buddy in fact has led this ragtag fugitive fleet into the woods, and together, they have found me. Hmm, maybe I misjudged Buddy. His heart is in the right place—it's his mind that always seems to be somewhere else. His manners could also use some… Nope, I'm not going to go there right now. I'm happy to be up and out of that dreadful den I was in, and somehow Buddy is the one who led the charge. Today he put his best paw forward, and I will do the same.

"Thanks to all of you for helping a girl out of a tough spot this afternoon," I bark to the group. "Looking around, I don't know all of you quite yet, but together, we sure make up one motley looking crew." Turning to Buddy, I say, "I may only tell this to you once, but thanks, little brother. I was pretty worried for a bit, but somehow knew that if anyone was going to find me, it was going to be you." Working to not show any emotion, or a tear, I quickly change the subject. "Seahawks look to have a good team this year. Go Hawks!"

"You're welcome," says Buddy.

Buddy chats with his two new friends, the deer, who he seems to be calling AH1 and AH2. Taking a moment for myself, I look around to try and figure out where we are. The sun has started to set, and with darkness coming quicker this time of year, we don't have much light left to find our way home.

"Okay, everybody, huddle up," I say to the crew. "My brother and I have been gone for quite some time and will need to get going soon if we are to make it home before dark. I believe my parentals are searching for us, so the sooner we get back, the better it will be for the two of us. But in all the confusion, I'm not sure where we are, or how to get back. Any thoughts?"

Buddy walks right over to me and sniffs my head. "What the what?" I ask.

"I needed to get Mom's scent off of you to help find the way," Buddy says. "Plus, I like messing with you."

Buddy turns to the deer and nods as if some secret code had just been detected. "Well, did it work?" I ask.

"Yep, I got Mom's scent and Pops's."

Time to rock and roll. I leave the wreckage of my past behind me and start to head up a slight incline, ready to return home and see Mom and

Dad. Okay, anything resembling inclines right now just won't do. Staying on solid, flat ground is quite fine with me. Being outside on my own today was fun, but I don't think I want to make this my permanent gig. I need to learn not to push things too far. Buddy quickly joins me. I can't head out without a final word to my new pack.

"Fellas," I say. "I consider myself lucky. Not just because of the rescue, for which I'm eternally grateful, but mostly because I've made some new friends. I've seen you all before from my house before and wondered what it would be like to run up and say hi. I'm very playful that way. Today, I got to do just that. I got to meet my new friends Ed and Al, and we shared some fun times getting to know each other while running from the deer, who, aside from getting off on the wrong hoof, I would meet and now call you my friends as well. I'm sorry, I never officially got your names."

"Alfred Hitchcock the first at your service, and this is my son, Alfred Hitchcock the second."

I don't believe it, AH1 and AH2. Buddy had that right the entire time. Maybe there is more going on upstairs that I give him credit for.

"Holy Smokies!" I say to the deer. "Hitchcock, like the director?"

"Indeed," says AH2. "Our master from back home on the farm used to always project films on a makeshift screen he would set up against the side of the stable during the warmer months."

"Awesome," I say. "My dad loves the master of suspense and I've sat with him many times watching the films, as you call them. My favorite is the one shot almost entirely from one little dwelling in a village housed in a magical place called New York City. I can relate to the lead human as I too have a tendency to look out my window at the goings on of my fellow neighbors but don't go as far with the image taker. Also, I do enjoy the female human. She has style, grace and beauty, just like my Mom. AH1 and AH2, you both rock." I pause. "Buddy, how did you know their names?"

"Most excellent, I just went with Antenna Head One and Antenna Head Two 'cause they have antennas and there's, like, two of them," says Buddy.

"Now, there's the brother I know." He never ceases to amaze, especially after today. "Anyway, Buddy and I need to go, but we do count you as our friends now. If my brother and I see you from our house, we will probably run to the window to say hi. I'm sure my parentals won't let us out as easily next time, but if you get the chance, don't be strangers."

"Be excellent to each other," says Buddy.

"Really," I say. "How many *Bill and Ted* references are you going to toss around?"

"Who?" asks Buddy.

With those parting words, Buddy and I leave the gang and head back toward the house. Buddy has his nose to the ground and moves quickly. Look at him go. Guess he is in as big a hurry as I am to see Mom and Dad. Oh gosh, Mom and Dad. How are we going to get out of this one? In the background, over the sound of our footsteps, I think I hear something. "Buddy. Stop. Do you hear that?" It's her! In the distance, I hear Mom calling our names. I hear the concerned tone in her voice. Don't worry Mom, I think, the two of us will be home in no time.

"Well, what do you know," I say. "You got us home, Buddy. Come on, dude, let's go face the music." At that moment, I've never felt more connected to my brother. He went against Mom's wishes and took it upon himself to find little old me. I'm pretty sure he's never going to let me forget this. I know I never will. After hearing Mom's voice, Buddy takes off running like a shot and before I can look up, he is gone. Well, that moment was short-lived. This last part I will have to do on my own. I see the backyards of similar homes in my general neighborhood now as I slowly return to the real world. Not sure if I'm going the same route as my brother, but I will use my senses for this last leg.

Being on this adventure today has given me a lot to think about. I think I know why Mom and Dad have a fence around our yard. It's to protect us from getting out and to keep strangers from entering the yard. The "rules" they put in place for us are actually for our protection. Our parentals look after us. To them, my brother and I are their children. They teach us discipline in the form of sitting, staying and coming when they call our names. As much as I want to be an adult, I am not. I still need their guidance and structure. After all, I think I proved that today.

Moving forward, I notice my surroundings start to change. The dirt path changes to gravel and now sidewalk. I've taken a bit of a detour, but I do recognize the neighborhood and should be home soon. Wait, did I just acknowledge that my parentals are right and I should listen to them? I hope Mom and Dad will forgive me. My parentals are very wise. Oh, and very old. They go to sleep around nine at night. Nine, who does that?

Walking down the sidewalk, I hear a low rumble coming up from behind. I know that sound. Quad port exhaust, menacing howl of the engine, rolling tires on the blacktop: that must be Dad's ride. Turning around, I see Dad round the corner in his vehicle. Dad stops the car, calls my name, and I come running toward him. As he gets out of the car, I leap into his outstretched arms and almost knock him over, I'm so excited to see him. My tail is no longer under my control and is wagging as if all by itself. I'm so happy.

"Sydney, we were so worried about you," Dad says. "Where have you been? Come on, let's get you home."

Home, yes, let's go home. I walk around to the passenger side of the car with Dad. He opens the door for me. Once back inside, Dad puts my window down and eases the car into gear. The vehicle starts to move down the street. I do love the cool breeze on my fur. I flop my front paws out the window and let them dangle down the side of the car with my tongue hanging out of my mouth. Home—that sure does have a nice ring to it.

CHAPTER 20

SYDNEY

DAD DRIVES SLOWLY DOWN the neighborhood streets. Wonderful smells waft from the various houses as we pass by: barbeque chicken, smoked sausage, just a hint of teriyaki sauce. I look over and watch Dad for a few moments. What is he thinking? Is he upset with me? Dad appears calm. What waits for me at home? As he turns onto our street, he reaches over and gives me a quick pet on my head. The soft touch of his hand feels so nice and comfortable. Sighing with pleasure, I settle back into the soft seat. I am headed home. I sure did miss him and Mom today.

The two of us round the final turn and continue the slow roll down the front stretch on our street. Finally, there it is. The charming little abode I call home. Looking out from the passenger window, I see my room where I do my work every day. My little window to the world. I sure am one lucky dog. I never thought about all that Mom and Dad provide for my brother and me. We have a woof—sorry, roof—over our heads, food to eat, treats to enjoy, and all the tummy rubs one little pup can take. FYI, I can take quite a bit. The driveway is full of vehicles and we park out front. I can see Mom's auto and a great white whale of a minivan. Dad gets out and comes around to my side, opening the door, but instructs me to wait for just a bit. He pulls my leash from the back of the car and clips it on.

"Not getting away from us this time," Dad says. "Come on, Syd, we're going to be late for dinner."

Nope, I think to myself. Not going anywhere. Wait, what, did he just say dinner? Dad lets me out of the car and we walk toward the front of the house. I hear the sound of voices coming from inside. I follow Dad up the three concrete steps and pass the potted plants that Mom works so hard to water during the summer months. Instead of reaching for his keys, Dad pushes a button against the house and I hear that familiar sound of the front doorbell. Ah, so this is where it come from. Genius!

"I'll get it," I hear Mom say as she approaches the door. In an instant, I hear the top lock of the door turn and the door swings open.

"Sydney!"

Dad lets go of the leash and I jump up into her outstretched arms. I proceed to kiss her face and wag my tail as fast as possible. Any worries I had about how she would react are gone in an instant. My mom missed me just as much as I missed her.

"Oh, Sydney," she says. "I'm so glad to see you. Let me look at you. Are you okay?"

Well, it's a long story, I think.

"She seems fine," I hear Dad say. "I think she missed us."

How right they are. On this roller coaster ride of emotions, today this is the highest of highs.

"Everybody, Sydney's home," Mom calls out to the other people in the house.

At that moment, Buddy comes running up to me and gives me a quick lick on my head. Yay, he made it back. I was a little worried about him after we parted in the woods. Glad to see he's home as well. I hear familiar voices, and the house is filled with wonderful smells. If my nose is correct, and honestly, when isn't it? I smell chicken and just a hint of curry from the kitchen. Mom must be making her famous chicken broccoli casserole dish. Yum!

"There she is. We heard you got into a bit of trouble today," says Fitz. "Are you okay, Sydney?"

Mwah! Fitz gives me a big kiss. She is the best. I'm so excited to see her and kiss her right back.

I do love Fitz; she smells like apples and that can never be a bad thing. If she is here, then surely her little sister Palmer can't be too far behind.

"Syds," Palmer says as she comes running up to the door. "Happy to see you home. I missed you so much." Palmer is so cute. She always likes to play and I have plenty of energy to keep up with her. Palmer likes to put my floppy ears up in a bun on top of my head and I sit there and let her do it. We have a special bond that way. What can I say, little girls and our hair. Can't beat it. She leans in and gives me a hug and a kiss. A girl can get used to this.

"Miss Sydney, there you are," says Fitz and Palmer's mom, River, emerging from just behind her girls. "Heard you caused a little trouble this afternoon, but happy to see you made it back in one piece."

I'm glad Mom made friends with River. The girls, what with their youthful glow, ooze positive energy whenever they come over and always brighten my day. I do love friends. You know, aside from me getting out and stuck in the woods, this is turning out to be the best day ever. I've somehow come home to a celebration. Uh-huh, that's how I roll.

As the dinner hour is upon us, Fitz asks if my mom can play a song on the piano she sees in the other room. Mom is a classically trained pianist, and plays songs for my brother and me when time permits. She doesn't play much for anyone else, as she says she is out of practice. But, with Fitz's insistence, Mom agrees and the group heads to the music room where we settle in for a beautiful piece by one of Mom's faves. I think she calls it Rachmaninoff, and Dad seems to like it because it has "rock" right there in the title. I cozy up next to Mom by her feet and enjoy the sounds coming from the black and white keys above me. She is so talented. After a few minutes, the song ends to the roaring approval of the audience. Mom asks the girls if they've ever seen a dog play the piano before. Looks like she's going for an encore tonight. Doesn't she know it's best to leave the stage, chug an iced tea, and then return to her adoring fans?

"What?" Palmer asks. "Can Sydney play the piano?"

"She sure can," Mom says. "Sydney, do you want to help me with this next number?"

Do I? But of course. I walk over to Mom and stand up on my hind legs. I situate myself between Mom and the piano bench she's sitting on and place my paws gently on the keys. Mom proceeds to play the next tune and I help by standing there and looking pretty. Okay, truth be told, I don't actually play. My paws don't quite fit on the keys. However, the fact that I stand patiently still seems to please Mom, Dad and the girls and what can I say, I'm a ham. Ooh, speaking of, when do we eat?

After dinner, the girls prepare to make their exit and I give kisses to Fitz, Palmer and their mom. With goodbyes from Mom and Dad, Buddy and me, the girls head out for their home. Dad and Buddy then make their way back to the kitchen, but Mom stays with me and says we need to talk. Well, I knew this was coming. I have to face the music sooner or later. In all the excitement of the dinner guests, I kind of hoped Mom would have forgotten my little excursion earlier this afternoon. Not so lucky, it appears.

"Sydney, you had your father and I very worried today," Mom says. "I know you're a dog, but I feel like we can understand each other. You really scared me. I went looking for you and when I couldn't find you, I feared the worst. Then, your brother ran into the woods to what I can only assume was to find you. I don't know what I would have done if I lost you both."

Mom's eyes begin to fill with water and tilts her head to one side. I turn my head to the other because I do in fact understand. I never, never meant to scare her in any way, shape or form.

"Sydney, there is only one thing left to do."

Uh oh, this is it. Time to take my medicine. What will it be? No treats for a month? Perhaps worse, no peanut butter for —gulp—ever!

"How about a puppy cuddle," she says with a big smile on her face.

Wow, do I love her. I run right over to her and we hug for quite some time. To be honest, I don't know just how long, nor do I care. I am back home where I belong, with my mom, dad and yes, my brother Buddy. I'm glad to be back here, home sweet home.

As the hour is now late (again, the parentals seem to go to bed early), we all head upstairs for the night. I follow Dad into the bedroom as Buddy hangs back with Mom in her office. Ah, Buddy, he never leaves her side. If you make friends with him, you've made a friend for life. I never understood that about him before, but I get it now. He may be needy, but he will be there for you no matter what. I'm glad he was there today.

I jump up on the bed where Dad is taking off his shoes. He reaches out to pet my head.

"We missed you today, Syd," he says. "Don't know what we'd do without you."

My words exactly. Dad gives me a big hug and scratches my tummy for a couple of minutes. He then changes into his pajamas and climbs into bed as Mom and Buddy come into the room. Buddy heads to his dog bed and in a minute, Mom joins Dad and me on the bed.

"Sydney," she says, "your dad and I sleep up here and it's time for you to get on your own bed."

I give her one last kiss and jump off, settling in at the foot of the bed on Dad's side without a worry. Then, Mom turns on the pane of knowledge. Sometimes she turns it on when she's ready for bed as this helps her go to sleep. I know I will hop back up on the bed later, after they fall asleep. My eyelids are starting to feel a bit heavy now. It's been a long day. Sleep starts to take hold of me, and I think about how thankful I am for my family. You never think about the little things day in and day out that make up family life. Those memories are somehow just there. Today, I took that for granted and came close to never finding my way back to Mom, Dad and Buddy. I know I don't want that to ever happen. There may be no "I" in the team I found myself a part of today, but there certainly is in family. Right where "I" belong.

THE END

Chris Minich is a writer living in Snoqualmie Washington. He enjoys spending time with his wife and their two precocious dogs, Sydney and Buddy. Chris is also a die-hard Seattle Seahawks fan.

Follow the Misadventures and stay connected for all the latest information

Website
http://www.chrisminich.com/
Facebook
https://www.facebook.com/ChrisMinichtheWriter
Twitter
@cockapoosyd
Instagram
https://www.instagram.com/cockapoosyd

THANK YOU FOR READING!

I hope you enjoyed your first misadventure with Princess Sydney and her brother Buddy.

If you enjoyed this book, please consider leaving a review on Amazon or Goodreads. Why? Honest reviews are invaluable to independent authors. There are a number of reasons, but the bottom line is that reviews help new readers decide whether or not to take a chance on a new book.

Please help me spread the word by posting your honest review of this book.

KEEP READING FOR AN EXCLUSIVE
LOOK AT THE FIRST CHAPTER OF THE
SECOND BOOK IN THE SERIES,
*MISADVENTURES OF PRINCESS
SYDNEY: HAVE PARENTALS, WILL
TRAVEL*

CHAPTER 1

Sydney

"YOU'RE NOT DOING it right," I said to my brother. How are we even related? "Try it again. It's more hold and release than duck and cover. One more time, with feeling."

Let's paws ten seconds for stations to identify themselves while I explain. Sometimes my brother is a very handy assistant. Over the last year, we've gotten pretty darn strong as a team. Always good for a bark or two, I've learned to put my brother in situations that benefit us both. And this situation *definitely* qualifies. Who doesn't love sandwiches? Especially my favorite, peanut butter and jelly. Delish! The problem is that Dad thinks he can outsmart me. On the day in question, a hot summer evening in late June, my brother and I had a little fun with Dad. Well, *we* call it fun.

Dad told me to sit while he prepared a PB&J for what I'm guessing was lunch the following day. I've watched him enough to know I'm right. Dad likes to plan his meals. When it comes to food, he always has my attention. I'm a quick learner and an "A" student. Ultimately, I will be his undoing—I'm that good.

The pending meal looked scrumptious. Dad started with two pieces of wheat bread. (Darn my wheat allergy. I can hear Dad now, "Sorry, Sydney, I'd give you some but you're allergic." I've protested this "allergy" dilemma to the parentals, but so far no luck.) He carefully spread the peanut butter on both slices of bread. Sitting patiently, I watched as he opened the stainless steel door of the fridge and pulled out what looks to be the "J" in the sandwich. Strawberry jelly, my favorite, and low sugar to boot. Gotta be mindful of those calories. I shifted a little in my position to let him know I was nearby and ready to be of assistance. Let's face it; I'm good when it comes to suggesting. Yes, I said suggesting; Dad uses the word "beg."

Dad scooped out some jelly with a spoon and again spread some on both slices of bread. Without looking, he told me that no amount of begging would do the trick. I'm sorry, begging? A cockapoo, certainly this one, does not beg. No, I prefer to think of it as "training your parental." Dad lacks focus sometimes but if I give him my form of "training," he catches on easily.

One of my signature moves is the head bob. I start with a diversion, like attempting to get up on the counter. Dad will tell me to get down from there. (Yes, sometimes I put my front paws up there to "test the waters.") This grabs his attention, diverting his focus from the main prize — in this case, the sandwich.

"Down, Sydney," he said to me. And so it began. I started with my head down, sad and lonely. "Syd, you look like you've lost your best friend." I slowly raised my head, the weight of the world so heavy it took all my strength just to lift it. I gazed right into his eyes and turned my head ever so slightly to the right, then softly exhaled. Boom, the head bob. He turned around and gave me a pet on the head but quickly turned back to the counter. This particular evening was trickier. Dad seemed intent on what he was doing and not focusing on me. Hmm, the head bob wasn't going to work tonight. Time to try another trick, the "but why."

If Dad won't look at me, I vocalize my needs.

"I'm so hungry," I said, pawing at his leg for dramatic effect. "But why can't I have some?" I watched him place the two pieces of bread together, then bend down to open a low kitchen drawer. He pulled out a clear plastic zip bag and placed the sandwich inside. He turned and locked eyes with him. Bingo!

"Syd, you've been a good dog. Want to lick the spoon?"

"Good boy," I said to him.

And that's how you train a parental when you're hungry.

Dad is funny when he tries to explain why I can't have food ("people food," that is). He will say, and I quote here, "I will not fall victim to your cockapoo charms." Oh, and occasionally he'll bust out this beauty: "Sandwiches are people food, and I'm a person. Sydney, you're a dog." I love that last one. Dad uses that a lot. My love for "people food" *began* with Dad. This is actually his doing. It all started with ice cream.

When Dad first began dating Mom, he would often come over for dinner. I was fond of Dad from the first time I met him. I sat with him on the couch as he introduced me to wonderful new programs on the pane of knowledge. Dad liked a certain genre of television program. These "shows," as he called them, tended to involve a crime of some sort, and he and my mom would watch together and try to figure out "who done it." It became a game between the two of them. The word for this type of show is "procedural." You've seen them. A problem happens at the beginning of an episode. The stars of the show are called in to investigate. An hour later the mystery is solved and you tune in next week for the next adventure: "Same bat time, same bat channel."

Dad would watch these shows after dinner and toward the end of the evening, he would get hungry for dessert. He would head to the icebox and, like the crafty cockapoo I am, I would tag along. He set what he called "ice cream" on the kitchen counter to thaw. I sat and watched as the container of ice began to melt right before my eyes. It was amazing! I did my best to sniff out this treat but couldn't pick up the scent. After a few minutes, he would return and use a scooper to move the ice cream from the container into a bowl. Then it was back to the pane of knowledge to finish the program—and more importantly, the not-so-frozen delight.

He made a point to not let me have any of the ice cream. I sat and stared him down the best I could. He was still new to me and I had to play it...well, cool. Finally, after his last spoonful of ice cream, he asked me if I'd like to lick the bowl. Um, you don't have to ask me twice. I dove in. I didn't care if I was getting ice cream on my face; I was in heaven. The ice cream was *so* sweet—a coffee flavor with a little bit of vanilla thrown in—perfection.

I remember those early days with Dad fondly, and of course that ice cream. This night, however, he wasn't budging on the sandwich. Sure, I got some jelly, but I too needed lunch for tomorrow. And so, we return to my partner in this crime: my brother Buddy.

Before Dad could put the PB&J away, I gave the signal to Buddy, who was sitting under the kitchen table watching the events unfold. Our signal, which I spent way too much time explaining to him, involved a quick lift of my right paw as I slid it just under my chin from right to left. Amazingly, this caught Buddy's attention and he stood up and started barking. He ran over to the sliding glass door that leads to our backyard. He sat down and tapped the glass with his front paws. Not only can I train my Dad, but my brother as well. He kept tapping and barking. "What is it, Bud?" I heard Dad ask. He left the zip bag and sandwich on the counter and walked over to the back door.

"Okay, Bud, you need to go out. Let me open the door for you." But my brother didn't go out. He sat there and stared at Dad. "Bud, it's hot out there and we're letting the cool air out. I thought you needed to go out. Okay, I'm closing the door — last chance." Before Dad could close the door, Buddy left the kitchen and headed to the rendezvous point. For our purposes, this was the bathroom.

"You're not doing it right," I said to my brother. How are we even related? "Try it again. It's more hold and release than duck and cover. One more time, with feeling."

"I don't understand," said Buddy. "I don't see the sandwich."

"Okay, watch and learn." Standing over the garbage can in the bathroom, I walked my brother through the steps. This can had an automatic opener. "First, place your paw over the blinking red sensor." I showed Buddy and the door made a grinding noise as the lid opened. "Second, remove any articles of interest in three seconds or less before the lid closes." The grinding noise began again and the lid shut. "Got it?"

"I don't understand," he said again. "I thought you got a sandwich."

"One more time from the top." I put my paw over the sensor and the lid opened with the now familiar grinding sound. This time, I stuck my whole head inside, bit down on the plastic, and pulled out the zip bag and the sandwich.

"You got it," said Buddy. "That's amazing!"

"Child's play," I replied. "Best part, Dad has no idea what happened. It's the perfect crime."

"Give it back, Sydney." In that instant I looked straight up toward the bathroom door. I could hear the sandwich fall to the bathroom floor with a thud. "But how…" was all I could muster.

Dad was standing in the entryway to the bathroom. He bent over and picked up the bag and left the room without saying another word. Oh, he's good.

This feels like a special two-part episode…to be continued.

Made in the USA
Columbia, SC
26 August 2022

66114960R00080